I0686006

The Girl with Flowers in her Hair

The Girl with Flowers in her Hair

Frances DeleCourt Winters

Black Lyon Publishing, LLC

THE GIRL WITH FLOWERS IN HER HAIR
Copyright © 2017 by Frances DeleCourt Winters

All rights reserved. No part of this book may be used or reproduced in any way by any means without the written permission of the publisher, except in the case of brief quotations embodied in critical articles and reviews.

Please note that if you have purchased this book without a cover or in any way marked as an advance reading copy, you have purchased a stolen item, and neither the author nor the publisher has been compensated for their work.

Our books may be ordered through your local bookstore or by visiting the publisher:

www.BlackLyonPublishing.com

Black Lyon Publishing, LLC
PO Box 567
Baker City, OR 97814

This is a work of fiction. All of the characters, names, events, organizations and conversations in this novel are either the products of the author's vivid imagination or are used in a fictitious way for the purposes of this story.

ISBN-10:   1-934912-80-8
ISBN-13:   978-1-934912-80-5
Library of Congress Control Number: 2017941860

Published and printed in the United States of America.

Black Lyon Contemporary Romance

Musette, Eula, and Nancy.

Part 1: Spring

Assemble the Ingredients

*Wherever you have
dreamed of going,
I have camped there,
and left firewood
for when you arrive.
~Hafiz*

Chapter 1

Her father slept with a loaded shotgun.

"Chasin' off bears!" he'd holler. "Or worse!"

Come morning, he'd eye the distant Kentucky mountain range, sniffing the air, looking for a hunt. He'd run his weathered old fingers through dirty hair that swept his ragged collar, and he'd spit a solid stream of brown tobacco juice into the dirt, waiting for something better than the dim future he saw before him.

When he died a few years back, her brother, Beeker, went straight for that old shotgun. Though for Beeker, sleeping with a firearm was a very different story. It was the two-legged dangers he worried about, not the four. It was the pack of guys and their unplanned visits, hunting for white powder and eyeing greed that scared him more than the pack of wild wolves, hunting for a kill, eyeing hunger.

Lorelei and Beeker were all that remained of the family, and she worked hard to keep them afloat.

For the past seven years, she worked in the bakery section at the local supermarket and discovered she had a secret talent. She knew what lonely hearts craved (hers being the loneliest of them all), and she fulfilled those longings with sweet confections that should only exist in magical kingdoms, not Bentfork, Kentucky. She quickly earned the reputation for being the most creative baker around. Though she was shy, a little awkward, geeky even, and she hardly ever spoke a word, her voice found release in her baking. And her specialty?

Cupcakes.

Not just any old cupcakes. No, Lorelei's creations were rich and luxurious. And the colors? Each creation was swirled with icing Van Gogh would have created had he painted in sugared meringue instead of oils. Plump and alluring confections, sexy and enticing creations—just the opposite of the short, plain, straw-haired woman who silently baked them, a secret smile hidden just behind her lips.

Her cupcakes could lure the coldest of hearts to the warmest corner of their souls, and those who were lucky enough to taste her sugary designs were rewarded with memories of secret longings they had forgotten about, warm desires they had packed away due to unfulfilled lives, and temptations that were too rich to bear, until the first bite. Some would smile with child-like recognition as they swallowed her creations. Others would look away, embarrassed by their warm-hearted memories.

A sudden loud crack of thunder shook her from her memories. The March rain pelted their tin trailer furiously, and the wind felt like a giant's hand about to rip the walls away and blow their house down. Lorelei knelt and tried to stop her hands from shaking. She stared wide-eyed into the secret box her brother kept hidden in the wall of the trailer—a secret no longer.

Rolls upon rolls of cash filled the old wooden cigar box, each bundled up with a tight rubber band. Stacked tightly like freshly cut kindling, smelling grey and damp, the color of poison and addiction. The rolls of cash were certainly cleaner and more organized than anything else in their miserable trailer. At twenty-six, it was the most money she had ever seen outside of the cash register at the supermarket bakery. She reached out a trembling hand to touch the cash as though it could disappear before her eyes—or sting her with a venomous bite.

It was real enough. The edges felt rough and dry beneath her quivering fingertips, sharp as an axe blade.

"You bastard," she mumbled under her breath, her southern accent heavy from years of delayed dreams, and she swept a long strand of hair away from her thin face. She didn't have to think long.

Beeker himself had face-planted over two hours ago in the

narrow passageway between the kitchen and his tiny box of a bedroom, and that's where he remained, thank God. Drunk as hell, and angry tonight. Real angry.

Or scared.

She couldn't tell the difference anymore.

She could hear his labored breathing, sloppy and rank as an old, wet shoe. She shook her head in disgust. Twin brother or not, Lorelei was done with him, this life, and everything about it. His drinking was the least of her worries. It was the drugs he sold, the late night visits from strangers trading cash for illegal powders and pills, voices shouted from dark-eyed, sunken-cheeked faces shouting in the darkness, "Beeker! You in there? I need sumpin' man!" A wad of cash rolled up in their tight, spidery palm, damp with sweat, need, and abundant hunger.

All over now.

After tonight's fight, she knew she had to get out. Two weeks ahead of her original plans, but she didn't see any other choice. Over the past year she worked hard to keep her move as secret as possible. The finalized plans she made over the past few months were in place. She just didn't foresee she would leave like this.

At night—

In the rain—

With only a simple note explaining her departure.

She always planned on telling Beeker, calmly, that she was moving, that she had saved enough money to restore Aunt Adelaide's old bakery way up north and that it was time for her to create a life of her own. He could have the trailer. But that was before she realized he had raided her bank account and drained half of her cash away.

She didn't even have time to pack. Not that there was much to pack anyway. She only had a few minor belongings, some clothes, a ring, a photo or two of her folks—nothin' much.

She looked at Beeker's slumped body in the narrow hall. Her twin brother had the same knack as Lorelei. He knew what customers craved—not the delicate cakes she created, but small baggies filled with fine powder, white as sugar, dusted in crystallized death.

He was getting worse too. Blackouts with a bottle of Jack

tightly wrapped in his fist, fearful eyes giving away the terror of the child he hid deep in his chest. Lorelei couldn't take care of him any longer. She had to leave.

Another gust of strong wind shook her from her thoughts and rocked their tiny trailer. The storm brazenly found the weak spots in the walls and sills where water dripped and stained the walls like the photographs of sorrow, ghosts of discarded memories. The cold, damp air caressed her face and whispered lies of unfulfilled promises, damp as mushrooms sprouting in the dark.

That kind of cold.

Her hands shook as she reached out to touch the money.

"Beeker, how could you?" she whispered again, shaking her head in disbelief. Without thinking, she reached a thin shaking hand into the box and pulled out tight rolls of cash and stuffed them in her pack.

She did it again.

And again.

And one more time.

She tried to ignore the tears that were running down her face, her heart pounding in her chest. Stealing? Stealing from her brother? She buried the guilt deep inside her and justified her actions. Didn't she bail him out of jail, twice? Didn't she pay all of the bills on their meager lives? Car repairs, speeding tickets, even the occasional loan. *C'mon Lorelei! Couldn't get work this week, you know that. C'mon Lala, Just give enough for a bottle of Jack at least!*

Unused to the rage she was feeling, she swiped her arm across her face, erasing the tears she refused to believe were from guilt.

Angrily, she stuffed one more fistful of cash into her backpack.

An explosive burst of thunder shook her from her task and she sank back on her heels. Defeated by the night, the fight with her brother left her weak and shaken, but the discovery of his secret cash was pure adrenalin—a feeling she had never known before.

By midnight, Beeker's stash was reduced by half. From her pocket, she took the folded note she had written an hour earlier and tossed it on his bed. She crammed the old box back into Beeker's no-longer-secret hiding place in the wall, wiped her hands down her old cotton print dress, and stood up.

She was ready.

She looked around the filthy room without regret. Trapped by the walls that restrained her for too long, she slung her pack over her shoulder and stepped into the narrow hallway. Beeker hadn't moved in two hours. He lay where he had fallen earlier, his face flat against the cold floor. The cut on his forehead had dried leaving a brick-red smear of blood, like the stain of an angry slap across his face. His breathing was deep and labored. He smelled sour, the way boys do, and musty, like a young man's life stalled mid-sentence and soaked in stale rainwater. She looked down at him. He had become so lost to her. His life was wasted among the cauldron full of toxic friends and poisoned powders. She shook her head in disgust. It took her too long to realize she couldn't save him—so she decided to save herself.

Tonight.

She stepped over his prone body, not worried about waking him at all. The bottle of Jack emptied deep into his gullet had seen to that. Leaning against the thin partition that served as a wall, she maneuvered through the hallway like a silent acrobat, sure of her space and determined to reach the other side, no matter what it held.

Grabbing her coat, keys, dog-eared paperback, and the old pillowcase she used as a suitcase, she took one last look at her brother.

"Beeker!" she called, "Beeker, you hear me?"

A mumbled reply from the young man was lost in the shadowy space between the floor and wall.

"Beeker, I'm leaving. I'm going away. Don't know what you're gonna do, but I'm done," she said tentatively. "The trailer is yours. I never had much here anyway."

She opened the thin door and looked out into the stormy night that swept over the mountain range. Dark and wet, it had to be this way, didn't it?

"Take care 'a yourself, okay? I can't do it for you anymore. I just can't," she stated firmly. "I found your money, you hear me? I took half. You hear me? Beeker? I took half your cash. Figure you owe it to me." She waited for a reply she knew would never come. "I'll pay you back. Someday, who knows. Maybe not." She took a small breath, unsure how to continue. "I'm sorry ..." And she jumped into the wet night.

Her feet slapped against the muddy yard as she ran to her old VW bug. Was she really leaving like this? She had planned this trip for months, but never thought it would end this way. Beeker passed out drunk and her pack filled with stolen cash, and wet rain plastering her thin hair to her neck.

If all went according to plan, she'd restore her aunt's old bakery in the small New England town of Cobweb Corners, serve coffee and cupcakes, and for once in her life, discover the serenity so many of her favorite paperback novels wrote about.

She tossed her pack into the back seat of the bug, and threw herself into the front. Quickly tossing the car into gear like it was a gangster's get-away car, she was about to pull out of the mud-soaked driveway when she saw Bear. His wet snout peeking out from under the trailer, hidden from the rain. The old hound dog was, in theory, Beeker's, but he never paid the old mutt any attention. The dog lived outside and frequently had to fend for himself, like they all had to do.

She paused for a second.

The windshield wipers beat a rhythmic pattern through the rain as Lorelei stared at the wet dog's snout.

She shivered in the dampness and watched the old hound sniff the wet night air, and for the second time that night, Lorelei took another risk.

She thrust open the passenger door and shouted into the night, "Well, c'mon then! Get outta that rain, Bear!"

With a quick bolt rare for a hound his age, Bear ran through the muddy yard, dodging the tipped plastic chair and trash can and leapt into the VW, smelling all wet and woolly. With a sloppy lick, Bear covered her cheek in one long dog kiss, sat down, and was ready for the adventure. His wagging tail kept perfect beat with the old bug's wipers.

Lorelei paused. A dog? Really? She never planned on taking the dog with her, but then again, she never planned on a pack full of cash either. She never planned on running away from Bentfork, Kentucky this way.

She took a deep breath. "So, you ol' mutt, you coming with me, Bear? Huh?" And she rubbed his grateful, wet head, relieved to have a companion for her new life.

She tried to ignore her shaking fingers as she pulled the crumpled envelope from her pack and looked through the contents one last time. A handwritten letter in Aunt Adelaide's shaky scrawl was stuffed on top of a faded photo of her far away aunt, and the deed proving the property was indeed, left to Lorelei. And finally, a map showing the route from Bentfork, Kentucky to Cobweb Corners, New Hampshire—a fifteen-hour drive. The rusted paper clip had held the documents together so long it left a brick brown stain of rust on the letter, an obscene watermark that hinted of dreams delayed too long.

She pressed the clutch, put the car in gear, and slowly drove away. There was no need to hurry from this life, for she was leaving nothing behind, but when she realized what she was driving toward, she pressed the gas pedal a little harder and a small smile crept across her softening face.

The storm seemed miles away.

The morning broke, dismal and wet. Fog hung in the valley thicker than dirty oil on a wet wool blanket. Beeker stumbled to the doorway, blinked into the blinding morning and looked over the muddy yard. His brain ached like a dry battlefield, and his sour stomach was filled with the bitter bile of twenty-six years of castrated rage. Lorelei's crumpled letter was held his fist, letting him know she'd gone, she was done with him, no more rescues (whatever that meant) and no forwarding address.

He was stunned stupid.

She'd be back. He knew it. She wasn't strong enough to make it on her own. Anywhere. Too damn shy, too damn weird, and ain't nobody ever come looking for her neither.

He spit into the mud. Last nights's rain had made the yard a mess and a thin river of muddy water snaked around the overflowing trash can and was lost under the trailer.

"Bear!" he called out. "Bear, you hear me, dawg?"

No answer.

"Bear! Let's go! Huntin' time!" He turned and ran back to his room to grab the shotgun. He pulled the sheets back and saw the board missing from the wall next to his bed. His heart froze.

The cash box. She found it.

"No, oh no!" He frantically searched through the pile of dirty blankets and crumpled bedding looking for the missing rolls of cash. "Oh Lala, no! Lorelei, you didn't."

Panicked, he ran to the door and looked out into the endless hills.

"Bear!" he called desperately.

A roll of distant thunder was his only reply.

Chapter 2

The sun had begun to set and darkness was creeping over the seaside town of Cobweb Corners. Exhausted from the near twenty-two-hour drive—she had only planned on fifteen, but weariness took over and she slept along the way—she drove slowly up Old Newport Road. Aunt Adelaide's bakery was the last house on the deserted road. She parked the car in the street and stared wide-eyed at what was to be her new home.

The bakery was just outside of the town proper and sat on the only road that led to the bay. In the distance, she could see the dim outline of an old lighthouse silhouetted against the dying light. Gently, as if to avoid waking unseen sleepers, she got out of the VW and stretched her legs. Listening closely, she could hear the muffled roar of the ocean waves hitting the shore. She closed her eyes.

"Bear," she whispered, "you hear that? That's the ocean, boy. We're that close."

Eyes closed, she breathed deeply and noticed the familiar pine scent of home was different up north. It was tinged with a sharper saline edge. Soft juniper tones underlined the scent of the sea, salty and wet. She turned to face the old lighthouse and let the ocean wind caress her face for a moment. Cool and cleansing, like a glass of Mama's lemonade. *Oughta make a cupcake like that*, she thought. *Pink lemonade. That'd be real nice.* The wind felt clean, crisp, and lacked the humid smell of damp earth and rot that seemed in infect everything in her part of the Kentucky mountains.

She laughed out loud. It just felt so damn good. Finally! No one watching her with odd, questioning eyes, "What cha doin' Lala? Tryin' to taste the air agin'?" Stupid questions from wagging tongues. "Just listening to the wind," she'd reply, sincerely. "Oh yeah? It tellin' ya to wash that greasy hair?"

Stupid people.

She always did her best to ignore the cynical folks of Bentfork.

And she was actually telling them the truth. Her mama always told her so, and her mama's mama before that.

If she was still enough, she could actually hear the wind's voice, well voices really, all mashed together into one lovely song, whispering in notes no one else could comprehend. The messages were soft as wind across ice, and each gave her predictions that brought a warm smile to her face, and a shine to her shy eyes.

But Lala's gift was not for fortune-telling or predictions, no. Lala's gift was more rare, and tellingly, more unique. The wind song held secret lyrics of her gift for baking. Heart-held flavors whispered in the forecast, recipes to create, combinations never heard of before. It didn't use words though. Just faint scents and vague pictures that were gently carried on angels' breath, swirling through her straw-colored hair—and even on the most trying of days, they could create a soft smile to bloom across her thin lips, and then there were the flowers, too. Her Aunt Adelaide told her they were her special gift, but she didn't understand. She certainly wasn't gifted with looks. "Anyone who listens to the wind like you, Lala, has special days in store!" And Adelaide was right. Lala knew inspiration, and she baked it into every morsel she touched. And those who tasted her sugary confections found themselves momentarily changed, more joyful, and always returned for just one more bite.

"You got any more of those orange clove cupcakes from last week, Lala? Reminded me of home when I was a kid! Haven't thought about that place in years—" old Mrs. Reiley would say, clearly comforted by the momentary memory. And Lala would smile in return, knowing she had given Mrs. Reiley a sweet visit to her past along with a small, sweet cake.

"I'm all out of them today, Ma'am. But here, try one of these ..." And smiling like the Cheshire Cat, Lala would wrap up four rosewater and buttercream cupcakes. "For pleasant memories and happier dreams," she'd say as she wrapped the box in red and white baker's twine. Later that night, roses in her veins, Mrs. Reiley tossed herself upon Mr. Reiley with a passion that made her own rose garden blush, but not with shame. Instead, it was gratitude that flowed through her and made her husband weep with love.

Lorelei knew she was going to miss the favorite customers, but they were rare in Bentfork. People in those parts didn't have a taste for the new and unique. Hopefully, in Cobweb Corners, she found a place to settle in and create something wonderful, something she found through the call of the wind, and a knack for knowing what hearts craved. Even her own. She had taken care of her father and brother for so long, she never even considered her own heart. Lonely and unfulfilled, it lay in wait like a small bird fluttering under a thin cotton sheet, ready to fly.

A bang from the second story demanded her attention. She whipped her gaze away from the vast distance before her to eye the disagreeable shutter banging against the house with a dull thud. An extremely tall, thin home built in the late nineteenth century, it looked like it was balanced upon carrot sticks as it rose steadily above her, arching toward the sky. Looking upward, as if she was searching for the giant's face who glared down upon her, she shivered as she noticed the rooftop's jagged line.

Leaning at angles impossible to conceive, three chimneys perched upon three obscenely thin gables and stretched their arms upward as if craving the warmth of a sun that had set a decade ago. Adorning each gable was a triple-spoked, cast iron lightening rod, a gothic weapon for unseen gods who perched upon the towering roof.

Home?

Lorelei's eyes lowered to the skeletal lines of the second floor that looked like it was about to buckle and explode. The weight of the story above it pressed downward with the power of granite and gravity, while below, the earth seemed to be pushing the ground floor up, up up, out of the very earth herself. Like a heavy custard sandwiched between two over-baked Victoria sponges, the middle story threatened to explode from its weighty prison with an obscene plop. Bulging shutters framed tall windows that looked down upon the small woman on the ground, daring her to stare a moment longer, and they won.

They really did.

Lorelei quickly shifted her gaze to the old front porch. At one time, that porch could seat about ten people, but on this particular evening, it looked as though it would collapse under the weight of just her dog. The bakery itself was located just beyond the double doors in the center of the porch and the old Victorian home towered dizzily above. Hanging from the toothy porch roof was a faded sign that read *Aunt Adelaide's Baked Goods.* And in smaller script just below it, faded nearly into ghostly type, it read, *Confections for the Heart.* Its loving message was a stark contrast to the building it had become.

What stood before her looked like the house in Aunt Adelaide's photo. Yet in person, disappointment seemed to ooze from its clapboard siding as it chuffed shallow breaths of used and discarded hope. For a moment, Lorelei felt like she was looking in a mirror.

Weak-kneed and exhausted, she grabbed her pillowcase of belongings. Fearful of waking the house that seemed to be watching her from behind a dozen eyeless windows, she walked quietly toward her new home. Bear followed.

Why was she suddenly so mousy?

She took a few steps.

There it was, only ten feet away.

Is this what freedom felt like? So vast and empty?

Six feet.

Am I alone?

Three more feet.

The empty building seemed to lean forward to such an extent, she would be crushed under its weight of repression. Faded pink and green paint clung to the dry clapboard like dried icing on a forgotten wedding cake. It must have been a beauty in its day. But now?

She sighed deeply and rubbed the old hound's head for comfort.

Fee fi fo fum …
It's so large, she thought, *it could eat me up.*

Challenging the cold stare of the house, she glared. (Perhaps Gretel did too. Maybe Gretel saw the threat in the witch's gingerbread house and was still brave enough to feast, rescue her brother, defeat the witch, and share the bounty with the villagers as well). The thought warmed her and a small smile crept onto her lips.

She lifted her fingertips to her mouth and couldn't help but whisper an extended, "Ohhhh myyyyy. Bear! You see this?" she cooed gently to the old hound. "This is our home, boy, our new home…" She knew she'd have work to do and repairs to make. She just didn't think the house would be so overwhelmingly gloomy, like something out of a child's ghost story. She paid a year advance in taxes, thank goodness, before that lousy Beeker raided her savings. A setback, for sure, but the supply of stolen cash made her feel a bit more secure, though it was cursed — blood money. Have to hide it away somewhere. Submerge it where it would lay still, under the bed, under the floorboards, deep in a closet and forgotten under a cloud of memories she knew she had to kill.

She shook the troubling thoughts from her head as Bear sniffed around his new surroundings. She found a home away from her brother, her loneliness, her frustrated attempts at a life. But more than that, she found a place to create, to grow, and to finally begin a life that had been put on hold for so long.

A home.

"Well Bear? Just me and you now. How 'bout it?" Taking a deep breath, Lorelei headed up the wide porch steps like a five-star general, but felt more like a mouse. The old mutt followed behind as each step creaked under the weight of a stranger's footsteps. The boards, though dry and weather worn, welcomed this new stranger and the porch posts, though warped with age, stood a bit straighter this evening in honor of this magical woman's arrival. They knew, and welcomed her. But the windows, who watched every step, reflected nothing but dark, empty air.

Walking along the porch, she gently stroked the weathered siding with her fingertips, boards that looked as though they had withstood a century of storms, and they shivered under her tickling touch, shedding a few old paint chips, which sifted upon the floor, the dandruff of a dying giant.

She reached forward and grabbed the screen door knob. It squealed open on rusty hinges, slightly resisting her tug with a fixed, tight spring. Lala noticed the screens, though in need of repair, were tinged with a mossy patina. Copper? Were these actually old copper screens? A breeze from the ocean swept by, brushing her hair with a gentle welcome and set the *Aunt Adelaide's Baked Goods* sign swinging with a soft song of squeaky rust and age. Lorelei's mind suddenly swirled with colors and new flavors as she gazed upon the ancient weave of the old copper screens—lime and lichen, spiced rum raisin, citrus creole, salted caramel and black cherry. It was always like this. She could never tell when the wind would arrive, but when it did, she listened and her mouth watered a little as the first recipe in her new home was written across her face. Have to write this down right away!

She held the door open with her shoulder as she fumbled for her keys.

The key!

Her heart sank. Hard. Like a rock down a dry well, it landed with a sickening thud in the toxic mud below.

The key to the bakery was in Bentfork, Kentucky. She was in such a rush to leave, she left the key under her mattress where she had hidden it for two years.

"Ohh—oh Bear, oh no!" She jiggled the door knob desperately trying to get in, but the old door remained shut, solid and firm.

Hoping to gain entrance, she leaned against the glass and peered inside. "Hello? Anyone there?" she called, knowing no one was. In her experience, no one was ever there. She had learned to fend for herself from a very early age.

"Oh damn, damn, damn," she mumbled in a panic and walked over to the tall window on the left. She quickly rubbed away a small circle of dust and grime from too many seasons of emptiness, cupped her hands to the glass, and peered in.

The space was small, but oh, so inviting. Lorelei forgot her momentary predicament as she looked around the room, separated from her future by an eighth of an inch of old dusty glass. Her eyes swept over the counter, across the old bakery case, a chair or two.

She leaned in a bit tighter, attempting to see into distant corners. She pressed her cheek against the dirty glass and the window rattled a bit in its dry, old casing.

She jumped back.

Reaching out with a tentative hand, she gave the old window a gentle rattle.

Loose! The window was loose, and though it appeared tall as hell, she could see the poorly rigged lock was more rusty than the screen door's hinges. She gave the window a strong tug, and though it shifted around, the old lock held. She quickly rubbed more dirt away from the glass and inspected the lock. It wasn't even a lock at all. Just some old brittle wire wrapped around a couple of screws kept the window in place. Hardly a security system at all.

Lorelei thought for a moment. No use trying her cell phone. The battery died somewhere in Connecticut. She looked around the street. Nothing in sight. No stores, no houses, just a lone streetlight and the silhouette of the silent, distant lighthouse.

"Bear, what are we gonna do? I am not sleeping in the car again. No way, no how," she said adamantly. Pulling her driver's license from her pocket—she hated purses—she thanked Beeker for one thing, sharing his illegal stories with her. Making sure she wasn't watched, like a cartoon spy, she deftly slipped her license in the crack between the two windows and maneuvered it toward the improvised wire lock. Wiggling the plastic card a bit, she leaned her cheek against the dirty glass, huffing a little as she slid it through the dry pains of wood. She reached the improvised lock in the middle of the panes.

There!

Easy as pie. Resting her license under the old wire, she simply pushed the wire up and off the screws.

Done! She shook her head in disbelief. It shouldn't have been so easy. Even the house, which had stood silent and empty for years, sighed as this charming young sorceress made her way into its secret recesses, welcoming the change it saw as good.

"Bear, don't you tell a soul," she whispered conspiratorially. The hound dog just watched and beat a rhythmic pattern upon the old porch with his mighty tail and yawned a garbled reply.

She gave the window a gentle tug and it opened an inch. No struggle, no effort even, almost as if there was inside help.

It's too easy, she thought as she made her decision. She had the deed, right? The building was hers, right? *So it's not breaking in at all, really.*

So why do I feel so guilty?

Looking around (making sure no one saw), she raised the window. Suddenly, it flew open and out of her hands, aided by the mighty weights in the old casement (and a little help from the old house itself, which had been watching her all along).

She jumped back in surprise. Bear gave a few loud barks to recognize the occasion. Swiping the dust from her hands across her dirty jeans, she tossed the soiled pillowcase into the room.

He put his meaty front paws upon the windowsill and Lorelei gave him the encouraging shove. He jumped in and instantly began sniffing the memories of the old bakery's floor that rose above him in a dusty revival of its ghostly past.

"I'm coming in dawg," she called to him and rested her hands on the sill. She squeezed her shoulders and wriggled in. Her hips rested upon the narrow sill. Reaching down, she supported her weight with her hands in an acre of dust. She paused, half way into her new life, overwhelmed by the sight. Through the old and acrid air, across the dry oaken floor, past the torn wallpaper and tipped chairs, all Lorelei could see were possibilities everywhere.

She wanted to call out, to anyone, to tell them she had arrived and was finally free. The smile that swept across her face illuminated the entire bakery.

That's when gravity won.

Like a guillotine, the old window snapped and crashed back to earth landing firmly upon Lorelei's rear end.

"Umphfffff!" she groaned out loud. "Bear, I'm—uhhhhh! I'm stuck—" The heavy window refused to budge an inch. She tried arching her back and wiggling her rump.

Nothing.

"Bear." She laughed at the ridiculous predicament. "Git on over here and help me," she mumbled as she wriggled in the window's clutch. It held her firmly.

Trapped by the weight of the window, her hands pressed upon the dirty floor, she kicked her legs with all her might, which just wedged the imprisoning window against her hips even tighter.

Half of Lorelei was in her new world, looking ahead, hands pressed solidly against the ground. The outside half was kicking at the empty night air, struggling against the life that held her back.

She paused for a moment and tried to back out the way she entered, but the window casement would have none of it. It held her firmly in place, determined to hold on to the magical intruder.

She continued her struggle as Bear sat and watched, wagging his tail at the absurd sight.

Outside in the cold March air, two white Keds capped two bony legs suspended above the earth. They kicked and squirmed frantically as another gentle evening settled over Cobweb Corners, New Hampshire.

Chapter 3

His memories were still too clear. Though Fran passed over a year ago, the thought of pulling the patrol car into his darkened driveway and silent home was a weight in his chest too heavy to bear.

He turned the car onto Old Newport Road instead. Driving out to the weathered lighthouse and watching twilight settle over Cobweb Corners always calmed his broken spirit. Those twisting iron stairs would last another hundred years, and the view, though isolated and lonely, filled him with the enormity of his universe and softened his grief. The air up there was purer somehow. Like the slap of smoky whiskey, it revived him, and tonight he wanted it super-sized.

The grief returned this week, strong and biting like an iron trap clenching his core. It always hit him unawares. A song on the radio, the scent of the ocean, a colorful scarf in a shop window—it was always the same. Unprepared for the rush of emotion, he would swallow hard and keep the pain suppressed deep in his belly where it festered like a cauldron of pain. Unable to stop the flood of memories, he mournfully replayed their final conversations over and over. A film too heavy to watch, but too sweet to ignore.

Their final weeks, the glances, the wishes and dreams they shared, he was unable to stop the film. Or rewind it even. He desperately longed for an alternate reel, a different ending to his movie, but like the advance of a heavy truck barreling down the highway, his film only unspooled toward one inevitable conclusion.

He gripped the steering wheel tighter and stared into the

dim future as he remembered her final wishes for his life, a life without her.

Eighteen months ago, he touched the IV drip delicately, as though he were stroking a soft kitten or a wounded bird.

"Chase," she said softly, "I'm okay, really. It doesn't hurt. Baby, go to work. The fellas are waiting. I'm fine." She looked up at her husband with sleepy eyes and pet his large rough hand at her side. "Just turn up the music a bit? I love this song..."

Frannie closed her eyes and listened. Joni Mitchell's voice was piped through the tiny, square iPod, and Chase could see Frannie's fingers tapping in rhythm with Joni's big yellow taxi as it took her old man away. The song never did make any sense to him, but Fran loved it.

He smiled softly.

Her cancer progressed quickly and with the few remaining weeks, Fran decided she wanted to be at home. She was surrounded by good people on whom she could count when the time came. She was thankful for that. She had some good days too when the energy returned. Enough to go to the beach for an hour or two, even a brief visit with friends.

Those were the good days.

Even so, Frannie refused to allow her body to control her spirit. She found divine release through her music. It always helped her to focus away from the disease, toward light, joy, the release when lyric met meter, when rhyme met rhythm.

Joni Mitchell was her favorite. And Phoebe Snow, too. And Ella Fitzgerald. The list could go on and on. Stacks and stacks of unorganized CDs all over the house until Chase spent afternoons and evenings downloading them into her tiny magical box, half the size of a credit card and more significant than a religious text. It seemed unreal that such powerful voices could be contained in so innocuous an item. That little metal square should be reeling and exploding from the power of the music it contained.

The only singer she asked to be deleted was once her favorite, Billi Holiday. She used to love the wail and smoky, roller coaster dips of Holiday's whisky infused voice. The sultry lust in her low notes, and the childlike playfulness of her high notes. But now, all she heard in it was a life of regrets, of booze and smoke, of drugs and disappointment.

So, no more Billi. Like a protective prince, Chase took the CDs out of the house and donated them to the library. Coming home from work, he could tell how his wife was feeling just by standing in the driveway. He'd get out of the squad car and listen. If he could hear music, he'd know, chances are, she was awake. If the music was soft, he'd know she was feeling okay, listening intently. If the music was loud, he'd hurt. He knew she was trying to drown out the pain from the meds, the cancer, whatever secret anguish was tightening its hold upon this woman he could no longer protect.

But then there were the days when the music was so loud he could flip on the siren on the car, and she'd never hear it. He'd walk into the house, and there she'd be, lying in the hospital bed they had moved into the living room, blasting the acoustic twang of the Indigo Girls. Her eyes closed, head moving in rhythm to some song about Galileo's restless soul and a smile as wide as the universe spread across her lips.

He'd watch her for a long time. It was the image of perfect peace.

The last conversation they had still left him reeling. It was just after breakfast and he was about to begin his shift. He approached her bed when she stopped him.

"Babe," she said, taking his hand in hers, "did you think about what we talked about last night?"

He nodded, thankful for this incredible woman. In awe of her spirit, diminishing too quickly. They had the conversation before, but Chase could never get himself to consider the possibility. Frannie, however, was clear. Chase was not allowed to spend his future alone. She insisted he date, he find joy and fall in love, raise a family—sooner rather than later. "You'll be the most amazing father," she told him over and over, with that knowing light in her eyes.

This morning, she continued softly, knowing the conversation was painful for him. "No matter what," she squeezed his calloused hand, hard, "no matter what happens, I need to know that you will find your way to being happy. That's all."

He tightened to refuse her searching eyes. It was all too much.

"Baby, you hear me?"

"Yeah, Fran," was all he could muster. He wasn't ready for conversations like this. Nothing in his ten years as a cop had ever prepared him for this.

"Baby, if I could, I'd give you forever, you know that." She smiled.

A squeeze was all he could give her. Words were not coming to him.

"But for me, right now? I need to know that you will be happy with someone, okay? You have so much love under that big badge of yours, baby. Someone needs it. Baby, I want that—okay?" She knew this was ripping him apart, but she needed to tell him. "Here's the plan. Okay? I want you to fall in love. Find somebody, really! It's okay. I want this for you, only for forever this time." And she gave a little laugh. "Got it? I need to know that you will. Chase? You hear me?"

She was getting tired. He could tell by her sleepy eyes and gentle touch.

"I hear ya, Fran."

"Good. Now, listen to me. I'm not leaving here until I know that you'll be okay." Her head was resting against the pillow and she turned and looked deeply into his soft brown eyes. "You want kids. I know that. I want you to have them, a family, the works. That, above everything, would make me happy."

"Fran, I can't— I can't talk about this right now."

She sat up a bit and tried a more direct approach. She knew the gentle way didn't always work with him and it was time for some tough lovin'.

"Oh for God's sake, Chase! Listen to me. I love you! Now wipe away the shit for a minute and hear what I'm telling you, okay?"

He smiled. He loved it when Fran got all tough and direct. Especially in her paisley turban. It was the best show in town, and no one else had the ability to make Chase listen the way Fran could. If the guys on the force needed something, they could always count on Fran to follow through. She had the strength of twenty cops when she needed it.

"I need to know that you will fall in love. Okay? I need to know that you will be a dad, that you will be happy. I want that for you. You hear me Chase? I. Want. You. To. Be. Happy." She squeezed his hand tightly.

"I got it Fran. I hear you." He lifted her hand up to his lips and pressed a kiss firmly into her knuckles, thankful for this magical woman.

"Oh God!" she yelled, "I love this song! Quick, turn it up!" The Indigo Girls were about to riff on Virginia Woolf and Chase just watched as his wife, no matter how weak the IV drugs made her, gather her energy and rock out or, as much as her body would let her rock out, to the heady, acoustic tune.

He smiled. In spite of the anguish that seized his core, he smiled as he looked upon the amazing women who taught him the very meaning of joy.

She opened one eye and looked at Chase. "Have a good day, baby," she said, and winked at him.

Gratitude flooded his core.

Hard to believe it was so long ago.

Eighteen months.

He turned the squad car onto Old Newport Road and through the gentle twilight he could see the silhouette of his grandfather's lighthouse. It was the only spot in Cobweb Corners where he could be alone and think clearly. At least once a week he'd visit the lighthouse. He'd slowly climb the old circular staircase to the top, pat the long-dead beacon for luck, and step out onto the parapet into the cool night air. The endless view of the coastal New England village always filled him with the serenity he desperately yearned for, and he found himself needing the silence of the lighthouse more and more.

The drive along Old Newport Road was quiet. Nothing much in this part of town except the old abandoned bakery—

"What the hell?" Chase mumbled under his breath. The dusky evening's light may have tricked his eyes. But no.

"What the—" He stopped the squad car across the street and watched the bakery's window. Two thin legs appeared trapped kicking in the air, white sneakers glowing like beacons in the night.

He felt a small chuckle rise in his chest and it felt good. He watched as the pair of legs twisted and kicked, clearly stuck by the weight of the window.

He chuckled again.

The legs seemed animated from within, driven by a frenzy like a wild deer ripping through the forest. The legs struck out at no apparent foe and lacked any kind of forceful direction that would lead him to believe the owner of the legs was a threat.

So he watched, and he began to laugh. Each pointless kick made him snort playfully, and each inept shove the bodiless legs gave against the air made him gaffaw, but it was the Keds that did him in.

Two white Keds, ladies, roughly a size six, straddled akimbo, hung in the air and kicked like a buck in a trap. Funniest thing he'd ever seen—and he began to roar, heartily and loud. He doubled over, gripping the steering wheel and howled into the dashboard, hands clutching the wheel tightly like a vise. Totally out of his control, he succumbed and let the laughter ring through his chest, free and full.

A rich deep laugh that was new to his body and brought tears to his eyes. Each time he'd recover, he'd look up and see those white shoes and pencil thin legs hanging out the window, he'd double up again, wipe the tears away that were blinding his view. Laughter convulsed his chest and filling his lungs with bright cool air.

So, Chase gave in to this rare joy. He sat in the patrol car and laughed long and hard—as two white Keds kicked against an unseen foe, trapped by a weight too heavy to bear.

He knew how they felt.

Chapter 4

Lorelei struggled in the window. Every now and then she'd pause and rethink her strategy, brush a sweaty strand of hair from her face with her filthy hands, and give it another try.

Bear was tired of watching and lay with his chin on the floor, sometimes lifting a sleepy eyelid toward the woman fighting against the window.

Each twist of her hips just jammed the window in tighter, torquing it to an unnatural angle, making the prison even tighter.

"Aw hell," she cried out.

"Something I can help you with, little lady?" The deep voice made her scream. It was rich and polite, firm, and slightly commanding, yet it was what followed the request that really annoyed Lorelei.

A suppressed chuckle. A hidden laugh. She heard it, and stopped squirming to make sure that it was indeed laughter.

"I'm stuck here—" She never got to finish the sentence for the disembodied voice erupted into hysterics.

"Oh my God! You're laughing at me? I'm stuck in this dang window for the past half hour and you're laughing at me?" She was furious and struggled even harder. Her hands pawed at the ground, trying to pull herself into the room.

"Mister, I am stuck!"

Chase tried to grab a leg, but the owner was kicking so furiously, her legs appeared multiplied by twelve. So he stood back and tried his best to suppress the guffaw he felt rising in his chest.

He failed—and he exploded once more. Hearty bursts of

laughter erupted from his chest and tears blinded his eyes.

"It's the Keds," he howled, wiping tears away with clenched finger tips and choking on his words through rich, baritone laughter. He cupped his heavy hands over his face, trying to capture the eruption into his hands. "The Keds! Never seen anything li—" He wiped the tears from his face.

Lorelei froze. "Mister, when you're done enjoying the show, I'd appreciate it if you could help me." She twisted furiously and the trap held firm.

"Ma'am, I sure will. Just hold still a moment. Let me just…"

She felt two strong hands prying themselves between the window and her hips. They shifted around a bit. A fist knocked against the window pane, rattling the casement.

"Lady, you got this window jammed tight," the voice told her. It was a resonant, too. Seemed in control, and had Lorelei been in a better position, say, behind a counter rather than jammed in a window, she could have recognized a hunger for joy through his explosive laughter. It sure was alluring though, rich and deep. Kind of exciting, too.

"Well, are you gonna help me or what?" she implored.

"Here's what we'll try. I want you to exhale, okay? Give it everything you got and empty your lungs all out. That way, I may be able to get more room and a better grip. Okay? Count of three. One. Two. Thr—"

Lorelei took a breath and let it all out, like the last breath of a drowning mermaid, she emptied the weight of her lungs upon the old floor and felt strong hands wedge themselves between her hips and the imprisoning window.

A bang, a knock, a hard shove. She heard the window pane rocking in its frame. The visitor pounded the window's four corners, and suddenly, two strong hands guided the window up and away.

"Oh my!" she heaved in relief. She scrambled backward like a panicked crab. Bear lumbered toward the open window, lifted up his head with a "'bout time" lazy-eyed expression and watched the young woman brush the dust from her legs.

"Sir," she began, attempting to smooth away the past twenty four hours from her visage, "thank you for helping me and—" Her eyes landed upon the most handsome face she had ever seen and she found herself caught in the most pleasant of traps—warm brown eyes under a richly arched brow, full lips that offered the hint of a wry smile, a chiseled jaw lined with a well-trimmed dark beard. She found herself utterly entranced when she noticed how broad and firm his shoulders were. He looked like a fairy tale fantasy. That's when she noticed the black uniform and bright silver badge pinned to his chest.

She froze.

Chase stood tall and firm, leaning against the tall window, one hand placed on the secure gun in his holster. "Now, you want tell me what you're doing here? Seems to me breaking and entering is illegal in all fifty states. I don't know about Kentucky, but here in New Hampshire, it could get you ten years plus."

"Kentucky? How—"

"License plate, Ma'am. I'm an officer. I notice these things. You want to tell me what brings you to this specific windowsill in Cobweb Corners?"

The conversation suddenly became real, a stark contrast to the previous ten minutes.

"Officer, I'm Lorelei Bradley," she said quickly, her nerves emphasizing her Kentucky drawl. "I'm the new baker here. Really! My Aunt Adelaide left me her house, and here I am. I forgot the keys back home and it was getting dark and ..." *I could melt like butter on a cast iron skillet for one of your warm September smiles,* she thought. She glanced guiltily toward the window and saw her pillowcase sack resting on the dusty bakery floor.

"Honestly." She spoke rapidly. The events of the past two days were catching up and she was close to breaking. "That's m' dog, Bear. See? You think I'd take an old hound to rob a house? I left Bentfork yesterday and was in such a rush, I left the key under my mattress in m' trailer. Here, I can show you the deed." Her hands began to shake as she tried to restrain her tears.

She reached into window and grabbed the old pillowcase bag stuffed with clothes and documents when her heart froze.

The money—!

What if he searched her backpack in the car?

Her composure began to crumble and she felt what remained of her bravery puddle onto the floor around her.

Shaking, she found the paperwork among her last minute packing. She held the envelope in her trembling hand and froze there, terrified to continue.

"May I?" he inquired politely.

Voicelessly, she handed him the envelope.

He ruffled through, map, notes, deed—all signed, official and ready.

"Looks like everything is in order," he encouraged her calmly. "Okay then. Welcome to the neighborhood. You're going to need another key unless you prefer windows." He smiled slightly at the joke.

A slight smile slid across her thin lips. She folded her arms and looked at the floor, patiently waiting to end this encounter. When she looked back at him, her fear flew away in the gaze of his rugged brow and a smile that had the potential to crack wide open when he joked. And clearly, the man knew how to laugh, and laugh hard and full of joy, she recalled ruefully.

She lifted up her face to him and risked a smile.

He smiled back. But there was something else. Maybe in the creases above his brow, or the slight recess of his eyes that told her he knew some sorrow. Somewhere, something weighed upon his spirit. She noticed it, and quick as lightning, she pushed it aside. It could wait. Something told her that she'd know more of this man, who could as easily appear like a lost boy in a man's uniform as he could a powerful guy just inches away from superhero status.

"Officer," she added sincerely, and trying to end the day, "thanks for your help." She smiled deeply and felt it warm her core.

"Sure thing, miss," and the memory of her flashing Keds ripped through his mind and he stifled a small laugh. His slightly convulsing shoulders gave himself away.

Lorelei noticed the corners of his mouth rise into a muffled chuckle, and she laughed slightly in return, embarrassed at her encounter, yet yearning to hang on to him a moment longer. She was surprised. He had a kindness she was unaccustomed to in the men she came in contact with down south. She decided to risk it.

She put out her hand, bravely. "I think a more formal introduction is in order here," she said. "I'm Lorelei, but my friends call me Lala. I'm the new baker."

"Lala?" he asked, somewhat puzzled by the odd nickname. "Really? Like in a song? La la la la?"

She smiled and held his curious eyes. "Yeah, like in a song. You just don't have the right tune," she said through a mischievous grin.

He shifted his weight a bit, and softly, easily, he smiled back as sweet as sugared icing.

"I'm Officer Chase Harris, if you need anything, give the station a call." He handed her a card and looked out beyond the porch into the enveloping darkness. "You don't get much traffic out here, you know. Tourists come for the lighthouse, though. Summer mostly."

Lorelei watched this man's gaze as he traced a path from her porch through the distant sea of grass and scrub pines to the silhouetted lighthouse. He seemed quieter for a moment. The path his eyes took from the porch to the distant waves, rolling in rhythmic meter, told her much more than his words ever could.

"Thank you, Officer," she said, watching his troubled silence.

Her voice shook him back to the present, and as he reached out to shake her hand, a wry smile crept upon his full mouth. Warm and safer than any wood stove on a wet winter night. "I'll have the bakery up and running in a few weeks," she said with encouragement. "Stop by for my house specialty."

"House specialty? I didn't know bakeries had specialties," he responded. Lala could see he was slightly prolonging his stay.

"This won't be an ordinary bakery, Officer. Though I'll fill it with anything you want. But my specialty?" She delayed answering just to fill his little boy appetite with a grown man's desire. Liking the result, she said simply, "Cupcakes."

His smile was all she needed to warm her through the next decade of winter nights.

He tipped his hat at the young woman in the white Keds

and headed back to the patrol car. Lala watched him drive away and swept her hand through her hair. "What was that?" she whispered to the wind. She leaned against the old porch post and watched the red taillights recede into the darkness.

Silence.

A soft rhythmic beat of distant waves called to her.

She took a deep breath and allowed stillness to creep into her soul. She closed her eyes and the sound of the ocean caressed her ears. A slight evening breeze swept across her face. New scents caressed her face and filled her lungs where they found a home like a long lost sister, happy for the reunion.

"Well, Bear? Time to explore." She turned to the window where the hound sat watching her. She grabbed the pillowcase and once more, tossed it through the window where it slid across the dusty floor like a baseball player sliding toward third base.

She put her hand on the sill. "Listen you," she spoke to no one in particular. "I'm here. This is it. I got nothin' else and you gotta help me make this work, okay?" She stroked the window sill with gentle fingers, and the house replied with a soft pleasant shiver of rattled glass like a tickle of chimes upon ice, too soon to be thawed and craving the warmth she offered.

She slid through the window with ease this time and looked around the shop. Not as bad as she thought. Needed dusting, some new curtains, a few new chairs. Wipe down the old wallpaper and maybe a fresh coat of paint too. But her heart sank when she looked upon the glass bakery display case. It was a grave, dead and suffocating. A glass casket to house rotting memories. Lala shook the unpleasant image away. Tossing the pillowcase over her shoulder, she called gently, "C'mon Bear."

Walking through the darkened doorway into the rear of the old building, she instinctively felt along the wall with her blinded hand for a light switch. Discovering the flip switch was almost instant (with a little help from the house's will), and she gave it a quick flick.

An electric buzz filled the air as the space was suddenly illuminated with golden light from decades ago. Three large lamps, the size of tiered wedding cakes, hung from the old tin ceiling. They bathed the room in a warm splendor that should have been accompanied by vocals from The Andrew Sisters — that kind of warm.

Lala cupped her hands in front of her face when she saw what lay in store. Glistening silver counter tops, shelves and shelves of mixing bowls and display plates. Old crockery filled with wooden spoons and wire whisks. Cake pans and bundt pans, spring form and baking pans. Fudge trays and pudding crocks. And leaning against the corner, a dozen muffin tins were stacked like the Tower of Babel and begging to finally be heard, clear, loud, and true.

As though it had waited for this moment through the decades of silence.

Lala smiled. Her magic could finally begin.

She swept her eyes across the enchanting room and saw the future spread out before her in sugar laced tints of rose-scented frosting.

Chapter 5

"Funniest thing I ever saw!" He laughed hard and loud, shaking the over sloppy burger, piled high in his hands. As he took another greedy bite, a blob of mayo and catsup landed on his plate with a plop. "Two tiny legs sticking out of that old window, kicking like some huge giant was swallowing her whole!"

Chase laughed heartily and wiped a smear of mayo off his mouth.

Connor howled and slapped his beer against the counter. He tipped his bar stool backward and lifting his head, he guffawed at the image his buddy described.

"Holy hell! Wish I was there, man. I really do. Any chance the dash cam picked it up?" He gnawed on another red hot chicken wing, its sour bite spreading across his face.

"Naw, patrol car was facing the wrong way. Best thing I've seen in a long time though." His laughter spent, he paused a moment. "Yeah, a long time."

Thoreau's Pub was packed tonight. Patrons filled the dozen or so tables as pop tunes piped through two tinny speakers nailed to the ancient rafters overhead. Sophie, the waitress, maneuvered through the crowd with skilled precision. A cocktail tray balanced over her head, she was still able to crack gum and flirt with the guys who caught her eye, earned her better tips too.

Chase was one of her favorites.

"Hey fellas! Can I get you refills?" She smiled broadly and cracked her gum in the corner of her painted red mouth. "Connor, my baby boy! How's married life treatin' you?" She snuggled up close. "Keighley is awful lucky to have landed a sweetheart like you. 'Nother beer, babe?"

"Sounds perfect," he replied. "One for my buddy, too."

"Officer Harris? Yes? Another cold one?" She winked at the handsome cop. She knew he still hurt from Fran's passing and tried to lighten his evenings. A free beer here and there, a special order of onion rings. Anything at all, just making him smile was a generous tip.

Chase took the last pull from his beer and agreed to one more. The last of the evening. He was thankful to be around friends tonight. An hour earlier, he had pulled into his driveway and his dark house looked overwhelming with emptiness. Vast and silent. He couldn't go in. He sat in the patrol car when Connor's text flashed on his smart phone.

"At Thoreau's. Stop by after shift. Let's hang." Connor's texts were always so short and direct. Not at all like the guy sitting before him. Newly married, Connor was the luckiest guy around. He lived with his wife, Keighley, and her grandfather, affectionately known as Pop-pop, in a large Victorian in the center of Cobweb Corners. Keighley was beautiful. All the guys on the force thought so.

Odd thing though, she read palms and believed she could see the future, or something like that. Even had a fortune-telling parlor in their house. Creepy. Chase never pursued the conversation. Seemed too silly—but Connor was clearly in love. Keighley came into his life like a breath of rainfall after an impossible drought. Connor's first wife, Randy, was pregnant with their first child when she died a few winters ago. Ice skating, a crack, and it was over in moments. Keighley was the healing balm in his life, and Chase loved her for it. Hell, the whole town loved Keighley.

"How's Keighley doin'? Any developments?" Chase asked with a sly smile.

"Not yet," he replied, peeling the damp label off the sweaty bottle. "We're trying, ya know? Which is great, really. But..." He trailed off.

"It'll happen. Don't worry about it. You guys will be the best parents around."

Connor sighed deeply. "I know... I know... It's just that—"

Though he didn't finish the sentence, Chase could see where he was headed. Losing Randy in her eighth month was a scar that Connor was just beginning to heal. The idea of fatherhood terrified him.

"Buddy, it's going to be fine. Keighley will see to that. Trust me."

Connor lifted his head away from the shredded label and gave a small laugh.

"I know. I got it. She knows, Pop-pop knows." He sighed. "How about you? What have you been up to? Have you thought about the dating sites?"

Chase smiled ruefully.

"Yeah, I though about it. Even went to a few of them too. Man, I don't think it's for me. They're all so—"

"Here's the second round fellas!" Sophie arrived with a loud snap of her gum and slapped two cold beers in front of them. "And something special for my favorite man in uniform?"

She winked at Chase and set a large plate of hot nachos piled high with beef, jalapeños and guacamole.

Both men groaned, and dove in like boys on Christmas morning.

"Sophie, You. Are. The. Best!" Connor mumbled as he stuffed his mouth.

She playfully slapped his hand and edged the plate toward Chase. "Well I already know that." She flirted back with a bright wink. "I brought these for Mr. Harris, special. And if you ask nicely, I'm sure he'll share. Wontcha sweetheart?" And with a grin like the Cheshire Cat, she disappeared into the crowd, leaving a faint scent of ruby red lipstick and the memory of another inviting wink at the officer in her wake.

"See! I've been telling you. Sophie just claimed you, man. Did you see that?" Connor laughed hard and loud as he dug into the pile of nachos. "Go for it," he garbled though a crunching mouthful.

Chase took a long pull from his fresh beer. "I don't know man. She's great and all. Just not into it, ya know. Somehow—"

Silently, Connor looked up at his friend.

"I'm just not ready. I looked through all of those dating sites you told me about. And—"

"Yeah? And what?" Connor swiped his hand across his mouth burning from the tangy bite of jalapeños and salty chips.

"Just not into it I guess. All those photos. People seemed so desperate. It's not what I want."

"Bullshit man."

"Huh?"

"You're full of shit and you know it. I can see it! You check out the ladies in here all the time."

"I do not check—"

Connor interrupted him with an explosive laugh. "Yes you do! You love it when Sophie pays attention to you. Your voice deepens and you get all cop-like! I swear, it's the best show in town. Admit it!" Connor was enjoying ribbing his buddy.

Chase stiffened. His jaw tightened and looked away. Standing up, he took a twenty out of his wallet and tossed it on the table. "I gotta go," he said and pushed himself through the crowded bar toward the door.

"Dude! Aw, wait a minute!" Connor called after him. "That's not what I meant!" But Chase was already out the door.

Connor tossed another twenty on the table and shouted to the waitress, "Sophie! Cash is on the table. Keep the change." and he hurried after his friend.

Outside, the evening air was dark and crisp. Chase was standing at the far end of the lot, stoic, hands deep in his pockets.

"Chase, man. What was that all about? You okay?" Connor stood a few paces behind him.

Chase didn't turn around. He stood firmly and gazed off into the darkness, at nothing in particular.

"Fine, I'm fine. It just gets—"

"Too much, I know. I'm sorry. I didn't mean—"

Chase took a deep breath. "Sometimes it gets overwhelming. I can't think or it all gets so tight that—"

"It explodes." Connor waited a moment. "Right?"

Chase turned to face his friend. "Right," he said quietly.

"Look, I didn't mean anything about those sites man. I just figured that—"

"I know, I know. Get back on the horse and all." He tried to toss it off like the good advice it was intended to be, but it still felt wrong, foreign somehow.

"Well, in a way, sure. It's time. How long has it been?" Connor asked.

"A year and a half or so."

"Right. And how is it going?"

"It sucks! It's sucks so bad, man. I can't take it. I don't know how you got through it. Stronger than I am, that's for sure."

"Chase, no one is saying forget her. You know that, right?"

Chase looked his buddy. Connor understood his pain more than anyone.

He sighed. "I know that."

"So, here's the plan. Simple." Connor paused a bit. "Ask Sophie to the cookout."

Chase stiffened, and Connor sped ahead with the plan like lightning.

"It's two weeks away. It'll give you time to chill a bit. No commitments, not even like a date, ya know? It'll be fun. She's a blast, and a good laugh too. Do it!"

"Sophie?"

"Man, she's totally into you. No one, and I mean no one gets the amount of freebies you do."

"I don't know—"

"Look. It's perfect. It's not like a date or anything like that. Other people will be there and if you get all wonky-like, give me a signal and I'll bail you out. I promise."

Chase smirked. "Wonky? Like, high school wonky?"

"Scout's honor!" Laughing, Connor held his hand high in a Spock salute.

Both men laughed and it cleared the air a bit. Chase felt tension residing in his core for so long that he forgot what a cleansing breath of air could do.

"Guess you're right."

"Score! My man! All right!" Connor's excitement was infectious. "Look, you and I will get there early. Dig the roasting pit, get everything set up. Keighley will bring Pop-

pop and Ruth. This way you don't have to pick up Sophie. She arrives on her own, so it's not like a date at all. Get it?"

"Got it."

"Awesome. Now go," and with a nudge of his head, Connor indicated a path that lead directly to the doors of Thoreau's Pub and into the lap of Sophie the waitress.

Like a general off to battle, Chase straightened up and instinctively felt for his gun.

"Dude! You're not going into a hostage crisis! Jesus!"

"Oh, yes, I am," Chase replied softly. "Oh yes, I am."

Chapter 6

It didn't take her long to fall asleep.

Once Officer Harris left (Chase! That was his name, Chase?) Lorelei grabbed the remaining bag and backpack of cash from the VW, ran inside, and climbed up the large center staircase like she was tackling Mt. Everest.

And indeed, she was.

Each step creaked a bit with her unfamiliar footstep. From the looks of the place, Lorelei knew for certain that if a stair gave away, she'd drop into a horrific wonderland of wildly anxious white rabbits and evil playing cards demanding her neck—or worse.

But the stairs held firmly and guided her along this new and unfamiliar path.

She spoke aloud when she reached the top. "Aunt Adelaide!" she called into the emptiness, "I'm here—"

Bear's heavy tail thudding upon the barren oak floor.

"You gotta help me, okay?" she called into the empty house. "I'm alone and don't know what to do."

The heavy tail thudded again. Thud. Thud. Thud.

The gingerbread house heard her, every tilted angle and sharp edge listened intently, but selfishly, gave no reply. It waited silently to see what this magical intruder could create.

With a determined sigh, Lorelei looked at the options surrounding her. A hallway to the right was lined with a series of old warped doors. Like a carnival house, any one could open to reveal a horrid clown or a distorted mirror, reflecting back the exaggerated self, out of line, out of angle. Out of spirit.

She chose simply. She opened the door directly in front of

her and found the jackpot. A large bedroom with two windows taller than the Kentucky pines back home and an oversized bed that sat against the far wall. The bed was mounded with pillows and quilts, as though it had been waiting through decades of starlit nights to offer her sweet respite from the storm. Large enough to get lost in.

Large enough to swallow her whole.

Who has been sleeping in my bed?

She shivered.

The room was twice the size of her entire trailer in Bentfork. But instead of a muddy yard piled with trash, the large windows faced the distant ocean. Victorian wallpaper revealed a romantic tangle of roses and daisies. Bright reds faded into soft pinks, and the delicate white blossoms aged into tones of tea stained honey.

"Well, Bear," she said to the patient hound, "this is it." But instead of relief, she felt diminished by the sheer size of the space—overwhelmed by the enormity of what lay ahead. She threw the backpack of stolen cash under the bed, tossed on an old tee and sweats, and pulled the dust sheet off of the bed. It slid to the floor like a liquid ghost where it gathered in a soft, cotton pile. She climbed into the gigantic, cold bed, and soon a small frightened girl in an overwhelming space fell asleep.

The rain set in early that morning. A cold and grey March sky followed her up the coast and broke over Cobweb Corners, turning the town's brilliant New England palette into grayscale tones of muted greens and wet browns reflecting whatever light was available upon the rain-drenched streets.

Lorelei yawned and stretched. Reaching her arms up, up over her head, she suddenly noticed the chill and retreated quickly under the blankets. Cocooned upon the pillow, she looked curiously around the room. The distant waves penetrated the walls and she felt more alone than she ever knew possible.

The old hound dog groaned slightly as she ruffled in the bed. Unaccustomed to sleeping in doors, he intuitively chose the luxury of the foot of Lorelei's bed. She smiled when she saw the sleeping mutt. He, too, chose pampering over hardship, the warmth of a soft bed over the hardscrabble life they were used to. Braving the cold, she reached out and wordlessly gave Bear a few gentle rubs on his head. He lifted the heavy tent of one eye, stretched a massive paw, and groaned a bit, pleasurably.

The rain pelted the window and ran down the glass in glistening rivulets. Grey sky and billowing clouds, rich and full, swarmed in the stormy distance.

She sighed once again (or was it a weak attempt to yawn?) for she suddenly recognized the enormity of her path.

A lonesome journey from the Kentucky hills to the New Hampshire shoreline.

A backpack of money she stole from her drug-selling twin, whom she abandoned and left passed out on the floor in a leaky old trailer.

An inherited house that looked like a giant dried mushroom exploding from an ogre's magical bottle.

And a hound dog, her only companion.

She turned on her side and looked out the rain streaked windows. She watched a tiny spider drop slowly down the window pane upon a magical invisible thread.

"Oh my lord," she mumbled in a slow southern draw, "What have I done?" The enormity of the move crowded her thoughts, and she shook them away, hard.

"Well, dawg," she yawned. "Let's start."

Lorelei jumped from bed and briskly rubbed her arms together, slapping away the chilled air, the old oak floor, hard and cold under her bare feet.

Grabbing her toothbrush, she located the small bathroom to the left of the staircase and flicked on the light. Soft green tile, old pedestal sink, and a stained tub that had seen better days for sure, but it was hers. Brushing her teeth in her own sink became a luxury as fine as a five-star hotel, so she tried hard to ignore the rust stains on the faucet and the crack in the porcelain sink.

She caught her reflection in the mirror and stopped brushing for a moment. She looked at the plain woman looking back. Red toothbrush held firmly in her fist, clean white paste bubbling upon her lower lip, she wondered what lay in store. Searching the curious eyes, which held her own, she was torn between two disparate visions. The exciting new life of the enchanted baker. Confections and cakes in flavor combinations brought to her by a joyful wind, or the woman who abandoned her twin. Left him on a dirty trailer's floor while she ran off into the night with his money and his dog.

She stared a moment longer. Brushing the memory away, she quickly splashed her face with ice cold water from the ancient tap where it washed the disturbing thoughts from her face into the sink. They swirled against the white porcelain like bitter snakes before they disappeared into the dark drain.

Patting her face dry, she called to Bear and began the day.

Exploring the old house was exciting—almost a mansion really. And although the outside gave the impression of decay and neglect, the inside—well, the inside did too, but it was different somehow. Nothing was broken, nothing was rotting or beyond repair. In fact, everything appeared to be in place. It was as if her arrival was expected, hoped for, desired even.

A large third-floor attic looked over the town in all four directions through squat, brittle windows that rattled noisily on windy nights. Below, there were four rooms on the second floor, and four more downstairs, including the bakery. A cozy first floor living room faced the street and a smaller dining room sat off the kitchen nook in the rear. A door in the kitchen led to the rear of the bakery, and another looked upon what might have been an overgrown garden in the back.

She liked what she saw and despite the gloom that rested in the corners and hid in the eaves, silent, capable, and knowing, she acknowledged deep in her core, that she could transform the old place.

And all along, the house waited patiently for her to reveal herself. To be worthy of the untapped riches she carried within.

Standing in the kitchen, she looked at the door leading to the rear of the bakery. Dry and brittle with age, it wore its hundred coats of paint like a badge of honor. Peeling chips curled away in secretive places to reveal voices from the past, its history revealed in period colors and worn away edges from a hundred other hands. Cautiously, she tugged it open and Bear followed behind. His paws tapped across the old oak floors and Lorelei was thankful for his company.

The bakery's kitchen was tight, but cheerily functional. She laughed aloud when she saw the large gas cast iron oven. Needed a good cleaning but it'd do the trick. She trailed her eyes over the space like a child on Christmas morning clapping her hands in surprise.

Hers! And with a laugh, she realized she had been holding her breath.

Trailing her delicate fingertip along the dusty counter, she spoke to the hound at her side. "Bear! It's ours! All ours!" and she laughed again as she peeked inside pots, crept through cabinets, lifted levers and pawed the pans.

Breakfast was on her mind when she was startled by harsh knocking on the bakery shop's door. Looking up, she saw a smiling uniformed man whose arms were loaded with a grey box, and two tall cardboard coffee cups balanced on top.

Walking toward the bakery store front, she whisked a strand of straw-colored hair from her face and looked at the man who appeared like a faded photograph through layers of dusty glass.

He waved. "Miss Bradley," he called through the opaque panes, "I'm here to apologize for my inconsiderate response to your situation last night. I thought you could use some breakfast. A peace offering." He looked at her with kind eyes, a sincerity like she had never seen in a guy before. The promise of hot coffee was more tempting than the man himself. At least for now.

She smiled at him and shook her head.

"Can't," she hollered. "The door's busted. You'll have to use the window."

He lowered his head a bit as he laughed at the memory, and her good spirit won him over.

"You can come in if you get it open, but I gotta say I'm a mess this morning." She laughed as she watched Chase wrestle with the window once again. The rainy morning suddenly seemed far away and she was happy for the reprieve.

He tugged open the large window that flew from his hands and rose with a clatter, shaking the casement's bones.

He hunched over and handed her a small box, warm coffee and clambered through the window. Standing up straight, he brushed the dust from his uniform. "Can I help you get that door fixed sometime?"

Her wry smile told him everything he needed to know.

He paused.

He got it.

"The door's not broken, is it?" He asked, a smile creeping upon his ruddy mouth as he realized the joke upon him.

"Nope!" she responded gleefully. He laughed full and loud. For a brief moment their eyes met and they shared the laugh together, enjoying the moment as new friends could, and perhaps they acknowledged something more. Something new lay beneath the surface of ritual pleasantries and the helpful formalities. As she held his eyes, she recognized that this moment was far richer and it warmed her core. New and exciting, foreign and desired, Lala tried to suppress this new territory within her. She was so unaware of her own desires that she never considered love. It was not possible in her previous world. However, looking at Chase standing in front of her with a smile that could warm a million ovens, those possibilities suddenly showered down upon her and left her breathless.

Opening the grocery store bakery box, she chose a pregnant, powdered jelly doughnut. She took a mighty bite. Its powder sifted upon her wrinkled tee like the soft snow of Narnia and she smiled as the jelly oozed upon her fingertips. She happily licked each ruby-tipped finger, enjoying the new thrills in front of her.

She took a moment to look at Chase as he lifted his plastic coffee lid. He filled the chilly room like a familiar guest, bringing the warmth of a good man with him. His uniform, dark and crisp, hugged his shoulders and defined his physique like a second skin. Lorelei felt safer in his presence and with a secretive smile, she wondered what lay in store for her—or them.

"Crazy old place," he remarked. He took a massive bite from a cruller. Lorelei noticed the cruller looked a bit too hard in his hands, dry even. She made a mental note. Crullers.

"Yeah," she agreed a bit ruefully. "Needs some work, but it's mine." Her smile lit up the damp room and she dove into her jelly doughnut, powdering her lips with the last bite, desperate for its sweet tang upon her tongue. "My Aunt Adelaide left it to me," she told him. "Only met her once in my life, and I was pretty little. Must have made a good impression though." She laughed.

"She was quite a lady I hear. The town was sorry to see her go. Some say they never had a decent bakery since she passed. Well, the Clam Basket in town has pies and all, but they're not a bakery like this old place was." He took a final bite and the cruller disappeared.

Lorelei smiled. "I'll change that," she said with a teaspoon of pride.

No, make that a tablespoon.

Her words hung in the air momentarily, and suddenly took wing. They floated through the bakery and into the room next door. They drifted up the old staircase where they caressed the banisters and smoothed the tea-stained wallpaper, finally arriving upon her bed where they lay like a tranquil satin quilt. The house seemed to grow an inch or two around them, pridefully, warming from her words.

She reached for another jelly doughnut.

"She only visited us once. Long time ago. Stayed for a week to help with mama. Then when my mama died, we never saw her again. She got into a fight or something with my daddy. Easy to do I guess."

"Yeah?" He took a warming gulp of coffee.

"My daddy was, well. Difficult."

"I guess some fathers are— Can be that way, I mean."

Lorelei laughed. "Well, my daddy slept with a shotgun by his side. That oughta tell ya something about him." She shook her head in disbelief, relieved to have left that life far behind her. "Anyway, I remember that visit like nothin' else. I must have been eight? Nine maybe? Younger? Well, whatever. She's the one who taught me to bake. Cookies and cakes, easy stuff. But just before she left—" She paused momentarily to get the memory in order. "Ya know, I think she was crying maybe, it looked that way," she said with a shrug. "She held me tight and told me I had a gift. A gift?" She laughed easily. "I thought she meant a bike or something!"

He laughed in return and took another large gulp of coffee.

"Mister, you're drinking the coffee down like a drowning man gasping for air."

He smiled at her remark. "No, no. Just listening, that's all."

Truth to tell, he was entranced by this odd young woman.

"Anyway, she held me really tight. No one, and I mean no one in our family ever did that. Kinda scared me like?" She took another bite and let the sweet yellow sponge and tangy jelly seep into her pores. "She kissed me on the forehead and held my face in her hands. She looked kinda desperate too, and she told me to bake when I felt lonely and she'd be there. But what scared me was when she whispered in my ear. I mean, it was, well—"

Chase waited. "What did she say?"

Lorelei held his eyes for a moment, wondering if she could trust him.

"She told me—" She paused for a moment and read his face. "Well, that's a story for another day," she said easily and watched the slight disappointment register upon his brow. "Anyway, come to find out, she'd been writing to me for years. Left me the bakery too! Couldn't believe it. Still can't. My daddy never gave me the letters, and when he died, I found stacks of them. Not surprised really. He was jealous I guess. Lonely too in his way. Scared even. I can see that now. I'm sorry I never really knew my aunt. Missed opportunities, you know?"

The house shivered in the rain. Somewhere on the second floor, a shutter gave a gentle knock against the window frame, demanding her attention.

"Thanks for the breakfast, Officer—?" She couldn't remember his last name.

"Harris, Officer Harris. People around here call me Chase though. You're welcome to as well."

The invitation was warm and welcoming and Lorelei decided she liked what she saw.

"So, what are your plans for the bakery?"

"Well, I'm the new town baker right?" Her excitement was

palpable. "I'm fixing up the place. No big changes though. Shouldn't be too hard. Can't wait to get in there and really start baking." Her eyes lit up with the thought.

"Excellent." He laughed. "Hope you make a good cruller, because this batch from the supermarket is hard as bricks."

"No nutmeg."

"What?"

"There's no nutmeg in them. I can tell from a mile away." Her smile was intoxicating.

"You can see that?" He asked, slightly intrigued.

"Well, in a way, sure! But, no. I don't see it. It's more like I can hear it. It's like sensing something's missing. A good cruller, a good cruller has to have just a dust of nutmeg in it. Just a few grains you know? Too much and it's ruined. Perks it up. Picks up the heat. Works like magic." As she spoke, she became more animated. She swiped a stray hair from her face and tucked it behind her ear.

Perhaps revealing more than she intended, she continued. "So, no, I don't see it. It's not like I was staring at your cruller and analyzing its crumb. I guess it was just, um, listening to it? I guess?" Insecurity crept into her voice. "Something like that. It's hard to explain. I know. I sound crazy." She laughed with excitement. "But that's how I bake. I listen more than I see," she said with a wry smile.

He eyed her with curiosity. "Listening to nutmeg, huh? What's the tune?"

"Same as my name," she responded with a magical challenge.

With a wry smile, she saw he was fascinated, but used to the poker face of a seasoned police officer, he kept it buried beneath his uniform.

"Sounds good," he responded. "As long as you can make a good cruller, you'll have a customer for life."

"Spread the word, okay?"

"You got it," and he decided to risk an attempt at her odd nickname, "Lala."

She laughed hard. "Mister, you still don't have the right tune." She held his eyes a bit, letting him know she appreciated his attempt. She looked forward to more.

"Hey, an idea." He took the risk. "Next month we're having a cookout, well a clambake really, out by the old lighthouse. Why don't you join us?"

"A clambake?"

"Sure. It's a great night. It'd give you a chance to meet the locals. Good people too. Only a handful of us."

"Wait a minute. Like an actual clambake?" Kentucky pig roasts suddenly seemed light years away.

Chase laughed. "Yes. Like an actual clambake. On the beach—with clams. We'll have a fire going. Sound good? Dress warmly though. Spring nights on the beach can be pretty cold."

Lorelei didn't have to think long. The promise of a cold night on a beach warmed by this giant's brown eyes was all the invitation she needed.

"Officer Harris," she said with joking formality, "I would love to be there."

"Wonderful! I'll give you the particulars next week. Until then," and he touched the rim of his hat, "let me know if you need anything." And with that he headed to the window.

"Chase, you can use the door," she laughed.

"No ma'am, I'm a creature of habit." And with a slight smile lighting up the corners of his mouth he was out the window in one deft move.

"Oh! One more thing," he asked peeking his head back in. "What's your specialty?"

"Cupcakes, remember?" she responded with a magical smile. "I bake cupcakes."

Upstairs, hidden under a bed in a dark, dirty old backpack, a roll of cash slowly uncoiled like a snake.

Chapter 7

Lala watched from the distance and let the sound of the waves envelop her. Twilight was falling and though the air was still, she had not become used to the cold chill of the New England spring. Wrapped in a coat under the colorful shawl she purchased last week at the local second hand shop, she stood on the beach between two new worlds—the bakery on the gentle slope behind her, while ahead, the future flickered in tones of fire-lit orange and red.

She watched the faraway faces glowing in the heat of the firelight. They were too distant for her to recognize Chase. She closed her eyes and listened for him instead. His laughter punctuated the rhythmic fold of the waves and smiling, she wrapped her arms around herself in new found comfort.

The weeks went by so quickly and she discovered she was hungry for his company. Not a schoolgirl crush or the instant attraction she read about in her paperbacks. It was deeper than that. Warmer and needed. His trusting face took up residence in her core and she was happy for this unexpected lodger.

She looked at the gathering in the distance. Reflecting the warmth of the fire in front of them, they appeared whole, somehow, and she longed to be a part of it. Not to be the new girl, but to be a part of their history, their magic and meaning. She never had a group friends like the ones she saw in the distance. She never belonged anywhere and suddenly felt awkward and shy.

The ancient lighthouse loomed overhead them all, dark and empty. How she longed for its light, a beacon to shatter the darkness around her and show her the path.

"C'mon, Bear," she said as she began to walk to the warmth she craved.

Six people gathered around the fire. Some in folding chairs, some stood, all with deep plates piled high with half-eaten corn cobs, potatoes and clams, crabs even. Steam rose from the plates like a magical mist, shadowing their faces in a savory fog that made her mouth water.

"Hey hey! Look who's here!" Chase shouted.

The group lifted their collective heads and cheered a rambunctious welcome. She could see a few beer bottles raised, amber and golden in the firelight. The group toasted her arrival and clinked their bottles like thick, clunky chimes.

"Guys, this is the new town baker," he announced. "Miss Lorelei Bradley."

It thrilled her and she managed a, "Hey y'all!" to the crowd, thankful that familiar Bear was at her side. The fire crackled and spit in front of her, reflecting its warmth in Chase's deep brown eyes. She held them for a moment and felt his gaze warm her core.

A beer was thrust in her hands. Strangers welcomed her with enthusiastic hellos punctuated by rhythmic distant waves and warm laughter.

"Thanks y'all," she managed to say. "This is incredible. It's so beautiful!" She took a small pull from her beer as Bear made his way through the crowd in search of scraps and a friendly pat.

"I'm glad you came tonight," Chase said. "I stopped by your place last week, but you looked so busy I didn't want to hound. It's really coming together."

Chase reached out and took Lorelei's hand, and she took a sharp, surprised breath. The contact was instant and the world suddenly stopped and fell silent.

The two looked at each other in wide familiarity and froze, acknowledging a mystic reunion. The party continued around them in sudden slow motion. Voices receded into the distant air while Chase and Lorelei were locked in an unexpected meeting, centuries in the making and seconds to fruition.

They stared in silent wonder. Small smiles creeping to their surprised mouths, for they recognized what others failed to see—a kindred spirit suddenly found contact in the warmest of places. A heart, a hearth, a home.

His eyes flashed.

What's going on? she wondered.

"I've been looking forward to tonight," he added, entranced by the shared warmth.

Frozen, Lala tried to find an explanation for her racing heart and she failed. She broke away from his inviting eyes and attempted to regain her voice.

"Same here," she stammered. "Been cooped up in that ol' place for two weeks. Needed some human company besides delivery men and repair guys." She laughed, hoping Chase didn't notice the slight waver in her voice.

She convinced herself she didn't need anybody, and so far, she was right. She was too plain, to short, too odd to find someone to love her. But tonight? It seemed her ancient theories were washed out with the tide from the moment Chase took her hand. She shook her slender frame like a pup emerging from a child's pool and tried to regain the balance she lost from looking into his eyes.

A young woman appeared at her side. Bright and cheerful, she instinctively reached out and touched Lorelei's arm, a kind and inviting gesture.

"Hi, Lorelei," she welcomed. "I'm Keighley. We're really glad you're here. This is my husband, Connor," she said with a note of pride. Lorelei noticed how the wind from the sea blew Keighley's hair into perfect whips across her face, like an advertisement for shampoo or perfume, a sharp contrast to her own.

Connor reached out and shook her hand. "Welcome," he offered happily.

"And this is my grandfather, Albert."

Lorelei smiled at the old man's kind face. "Nice to meet you all." She nodded.

"You can call me Pop-pop. Might as well. The whole town does at this point." He laughed.

Lorelei noticed he squeezed the hand of the older woman next to him, whose gaze was deep and warm.

"And this is his partner, Ruth," Keighley explained.

"Partner," Ruth laughed. "Oh my goodness, sounds like we're in business together. Hi baby, glad you're here!" With delicate fingers, she plopped a clam into a communal butter dish and swirled it about.

"We are partners," Pop-pop shouted a bit too loudly. "I'm in your business and you're in mine. The whole town knows it, so it's settled." Ruth dropped the clam into her mouth with a soft hum and a secretive smile, almost girlish in her effort.

Lorelei laughed. Though he sounded grumpy, she could see the twinkle in his eye that revealed a loving heart, and Ruth's obvious enjoyment of her meal was a sight to behold.

Chase interrupted. "Lorelei, here, let me fix you a plate."

"Come sit with me. We can chat," Keighley offered. "Chase, double up her plate with clams. I'll share! We're going to sit by the fire and catch up."

From the way Keighley said catch up, it reminded Lorelei of long lost friends who were just reunited after a long break, thankful to be together again.

Is this what home felt like?

A loud cackle broke the spell.

"Oh my God!" it called in glorious surprise. "My shawl! You're wearing my old shawl!"

Lorelei broke from the curious connection with Keighley and looked upon the laughing woman. She held a beer bottle in her fist, pink nails glowing brighter than the fire before them, and from her slightly slurred words, Lorelei assumed it wasn't her first beer of the night.

"I swear to God, that's my old shawl! Ha! Baby where'd you buy that?"

Instantly awkward, Lorelei tightened herself in the colorful wrap and mumbled a clumsy reply, "I ... I ... I was in the second hand shop," she said quietly, desperately trying to recover her voice. "And I—" she looked around the group for help.

"Holy shit!" the woman cackled. She reached out and grabbed a colorful corner of it. "It is! That's my shawl! Chase, look at this!" Her laughter was an unruly blend of scorn and glee. Mocking, and at the same time, sincere surprise. The combination disgusted Lala, like wormwood on cream.

"Lorelei," Chase interrupted. "This is Sophie. She works in town at Thoreau's Pub."

Sophie shined like an ill-timed spotlight, highlighting production flaws, out of focus, yet too bright to ignore. "Kiddo, I donated that old thing months ago." She heaved a beer infused guffaw. "Along with some jeans and a few fake furs. My Aunt Trudy," she said to no one in particular, "had rotten taste in fur." She took a long swig for her drink. "I decided to clean out the old stuff. Dump some chum. Out with it. You should have seen some of the stuff I was holding on to. Sweaters and slacks, jeans with rainbow patches. Rainbows. Ha!"

Lorelei sunk. She could never wear those jeans now. The patches were cute and they were cheap, so she bought them. She suddenly wished herself miles away, back in her cramped bed in a rusty trailer, lost in the Kentucky hills.

"Well, baby, looks good on you! Glad someone could use it. God knows I never could." Sophie staggered up to Chase. Grabbing his arm to keep herself from stumbling in the sand, she rested her head upon his solid shoulder.

Lorelei looked at Chase and Sophie and her heart sank. The waves seemed louder than ever and she cursed herself silently as the party continued around her. *Shoulda known better,* she thought.

Her night with Chase suddenly shattered and fell into the sand. She cursed her stupid heart and glanced at Keighley who was watching her intently. Keighley rolled her eyes, indicating Sophie's performance, and patted the empty chair next to her.

"Lorelei, come sit with me," she invited.

Lorelei attempted a brave face and sat in the lawn chair, tilted awkwardly in the sand.

"Don't worry about her," Keighley whispered. "She's loud and can be pretty brash, but under all the lipstick and Aquanet, she's got a good heart. Really."

Staring into the distance ahead of her, Lala shrugged. She never played with Barbies as a kid, so why did she think Ken would suddenly appear? *Stupid daydreams for stupid girls,* she thought to herself.

Chase plopped a bowl piled high with steamers and plump potatoes in Lala's small lap. They smelled rich and salty, and garlic hung in the air as the steam rose from the yawning clams.

"Here you are. Your first plate of a true, New England-style clambake!"

She tried not to look at the way the firelight made his chiseled jaw glow. She desperately tried to ignore the way the reflected flames glittered in his deep-set brown eyes. And worse, she tried to disregard her own racing heart.

"Thanks, Chase," she said.

She stared at the meal in front of her, overwhelmed by the options plied high upon the plate. Keighley handed her a small fork. "Here," she said. "Dive in. The clams are incredible this time of year." Keighley began to hunt through the open shells for a morsel of plump meat.

The conversations rose and fell around her like musical notes on a staff. She watched as the fire sent off a few cracks of burning logs, sending brilliant fireflies of sparks up into the cold night air. Wrapping herself tightly in the warm shawl, she dug her feet in the sand like hidden crabs.

Keighley's soft voice interrupted the spell. "Chase told me about your aunt and the bakery. Pretty amazing." Her enthusiasm was infectious. "I can't wait to see that place come alive again. It has been empty for so long."

"Yeah. It has been quite a job so far." Lorelei laughed a bit when she thought of her life with Beeker compared to what lay before her. "But it's home now. Think I can get used to it here. Really different from Kentucky, that's for sure." She shook her head softly and wondered if Keighley noticed her embarrassment, her dejection.

The two women looked at the empty house in the distance. It seemed intimidating from the beach, rising up, up, up, out of the earth, misaligned and incongruent as its newest inhabitant. *I know just how you feel,* Lorelei though silently as she gazed at the house. She felt a soft hand on her arm.

"You're going to be just fine," Keighley told her. "You belong here. I can sense it."

Lala appreciated her sincerity. "You think so?" she asked, wiggling about as she pulled her feet under her. She suddenly appeared a little girl. "That sure sounds good." She huddled deep into the shawl making it appear a giant teepee. "It's a really big house, and you're all the first neighbors I've met, besides delivery guys and such."

Bear let out a long yawn, hound dog style, and settled his heavy head upon his paws, warmed by the large fire in front of them.

"What are your plans for the place, young lady?" Pop-pop spoke up. "Seems like an awful big shoe to fill for someone like you."

"Someone like me?" She instantly felt shorter than she already was.

"Well sure! Slight thing like you, living in that old place all alone. Wouldn't let my granddaughter tackle something like that on her own. Little girl like you?"

"Lorelei," she said with a warm invitation. "I'm Lorelei, but friends call me Lala." She leaned forward in her chair a bit, a tiny head poking out of a colorful shawl wrapped thrice, and began. "Well, yes sir, it looks tough. But I'm up for it. I'm tougher than I look, I guess." Her eyes reflected the firelight in front of her and made her shine. "Life in Kentucky taught me that. So, I'm going to reopen the bakery in the next couple of weeks. Aunt Adelaide left it in pretty good shape. I know the outside is pretty crazy, but inside? Oh it's wonderful. Don't need to fix much inside at all. Maybe a fresh coat of paint. The gas company came out a few days ago. They said the old oven looks good, big fridge works great, thank goodness, and deliveries have been arriving each day, so I can start baking right away." She swayed a bit in her chair, happily anticipating the first bake. "So, you all can call me Lala, okay?"

"Lala? Ohhhhhh, I love that nickname," Ruth cooed. She clapped her hands and smiled broadly. She said it again. "Lala? Right?" Saying the simple name seemed to light up the old woman's face.

"That's it, Ma'am, you got it!" Lala smiled broadly.

"How did your parents come up with that?" she asked with a spark.

"Well," she thought, "I'm not too sure. I guess it's just short for Lorelei." Her answer was ineffective and hung in the air like an unfinished song.

"Well child, you've got to ask them! A name is an important

thing, and a nickname like Lala is too special. It doesn't come around too often."

"Nope, never," Pop-pop decreed.

"So child, you've got to ask them. You simply must," Ruth encouraged.

"Well Ma'am, that's going to be difficult," Lala explained easily. "Both my parents passed some time ago."

Ruth's face fell. "What? Really? Oh my—What a shame. So young. You're just too young—" Ruth attempted to understand the loss of both of Lala's parents and could only come up with a sympathetic smile that Lala accepted happily.

"Any other family, Lala?" she asked softly, concern creeping into her kind voice. "What about brothers or sisters?"

Lala froze. She had not prepared herself an answer to this question. Naively, she believed that leaving everything behind in Bentfork, Kentucky meant just that. No connections to the past. Beeker was a memory she hoped to bury under dark floorboards and keep him there, distant, submerged, and forgotten.

"No," she replied softly. "No one else. Just me," she looked down at her plate where the clams opened their yawning shells and mouthed in silent scorn. *Liar*, they called.

"Well, Lala, I am pleased you're here!"

"Jelly," Pop-pop grumbled.

"What's that dear?"

"Tell the girl about your jelly," he nudged.

"Well I—"

"My Ruthie here makes the best peach preserves you've ever had! Southern girl like you? Nothing close. We'll bring some by, won't we, Ruthie?"

"I'd love that," Ruth responded. "We won't intrude. We'll just leave some on the porch."

"That's mighty kind of you," Lala accepted. "It would be nice to have something sweet made by someone other than myself."

A loud laugh distracted her. Sophie was leaning against Chase's side laughing at some secret joke they had just shared. Lala tried hard not to notice the way she clung to him like a stumbling octopus hanging on a life preserver.

"Baby," Sophie hollered, "grab me another one of those beers." Her slur became more pronounced.

"What I think I ought to do, is drive you home," he responded. "How about it? Connor, hold down the fort."

Connor snorted a small laugh and tossed another log into the fire. "Will do, buddy, will do."

"Lorelei, I'm glad you came. Sorry to head out so quickly, but I gotta help our friend here a bit." And with a tilt of his head he acknowledged Sophie's stumbling body leaning against his own. "Be back soon guys."

"Aw, baby no," she pouted. "Party's just beginning!"

Chase looked at Connor who took a long pull from his beer.

"See ya, buddy," he said as Chase gently steered Sophie toward the distant parking lot. Connor gave them a departing friendly toast and sat in the sand at Keighley's feet.

Lorelei watched as her new friend stroked her fingers through her young husband's hair. He leaned his head back into her lap and with a warm smile growing upon his face, he appeared to sleep.

Lorelei glanced over at Keighley's Pop-pop. He, too, looked like the personification of genuine contentment. His old hands, grown withered with age, reflected the firelight in deep wrinkles, knuckles, and veins. Huddled inside those massive paws, she noticed Ruth's fragile fingertips, entwined around his own, like delicate vines wrapping a precious limb.

And in the distance, Lala watched as Chase supported Sophie's artless stumble through the sand, until they, too, were lost in the saline-scented darkness.

Part 2: Summer

Mix Until Blended

Chapter 8

Lorelei couldn't sleep. Though surrounded by pillows larger than the dozen flour sacks downstairs, the moon kept reaching her maternal fingers through Lorelei's window and tickling her ribs, or brushing her ears with gentle strokes.

Restless, she tossed, she turned, she fluffed another pillow and pulled the clouds of down up, up, over her head.

Lorelei...

Ump, she grumbled.

Lorelei ...

She popped open one eye.

"Bear? That you?" she garbled sleepily. "You okay boy?"

Just beyond her closed lids, her room filled with gentle light from the distant stars beyond her window. Giving in to the call that demanded her attention, she propped up herself on two wobbly elbows and yawned. A big wolfish yawn that on another face, could threaten to blow the house down, but on Lorelei, its execution suffered upon her thin lips and resulted in a mere sleepy, smacky, grin.

Lorelei ...

This time she wasn't dreaming. Something was calling to her.

Now? It had been weeks, months even since she felt that call. And it was always the same—a voiceless invitation that floated somewhere between her heart's fragile core and a soft whisper.

She smiled at the reunion—always unplanned, always unexpected, always welcome.

Lorelei ...

The tone had changed. It became more insistent and impatient, perhaps even a bit louder in its song. Heeding the call, she tossed off the toasty blankets and wrapped herself in Adelaide's own robe and stepped onto the chilly oaken floor.

A soft wad underfoot made her jump. Nearly toppling over, she quickly raised her foot dreading the worst. A dead mouse? *Oh Lord no, please not a mouse*, she thought as she grappled along the wall for the light switch.

"Bear, you mouse huntin' again?" she complained, but when she hit the lights switch, it was no mouse.

Money.

A tight coil of hundred dollar bills wrapped in a fleshy rubber band lay on the floor as if placed there by an unseen hand.

"Bear," she whispered, "you digging under my bed?"

The hound blinked in pleasant surprise, and the cash stared back with unblinking rage.

Confronting her.

Thief.

Lorelei!

With a mighty huff, she swelled her slight frame, grabbed the roll of cash and on her knees, reached under the dark bed for the hidden backpack. Perhaps it was no backpack at all, but a greedy red monster whose razor sharp zipper-teeth would nip, bite, and swallow her whole.

Fee Fi Fo Fum, I smell the blood of—

Determined, she yanked the dusty bag into the light. Angrily stuffing the rolled bills back into its yawning mouth, she zipped it shut with years of fermented resentment and tossed it back under the bed where it learned to wait.

In the dark. Silent and alone.

Lorelei! The wind was insistent tonight.

"I'm coming!" she hollered.

And she was.

She flew down the stairs, grabbed the ornamental banister post at the bottom and swung herself around the corner. She ran through the living room, into the back kitchen and—

Lala ... it sang softer than a feather, demanding as a moonbeam.

She threw open the back door and the wind began. Framed by the insufficient light behind her, Lorelei faced the ocean and welcomed the rushing breath on her face, whipping her hair around her and tossing the cotton folds of her robe like sails on a sunfish. She lifted her head up to the stars to listen, and smiling, she took a step into the dark, dark night.

It exploded in ribbons around her. The rush was immediate and oh so sweet. She lifted her arms into the air to catch the waves of scent and spice made of shared memories and forgotten dreams from too many lifetimes put on hold.

They showered around her feet like baby's breath and honeysuckle, filling her with a thousand and one nights of sweet inspiration.

She took a deep breath, held it in her lungs for a moment, and knew it was about to begin.

She had never felt more ready in her life.

She ran into the bakery and tying her aunt's old apron around her waist, she began. Throughout that night, a gentle dusting of confectioner's sugar settled over the sleepy town.

When the sun rose over Cobweb Corners that morning, Lorelei looked at the mess around her. Every counter showed evidence of her creativity, though she couldn't recall the night much. She swiped a stray wisp of straw-colored hair from her face, smearing a streak of flour upon her forehead.

Each inch of counter top was enthusiastically dusted with flour that looked as though it has fallen from magical snow-filled heights. Mixing bowls were greased with the curds of batter while wooden spoons stood firmly, proudly glued to their batter-rich sides. Lidless jars spilled their contents in a storm of raisins and walnuts, dried cranberry and cashews. A dozen spent icing bags hung limply off the counters. Like dripping witches' hats tossed aside and abandoned on a frenzied night-fly across a stormy sky, they left a riot of pastel icings smeared across their tips, dripping sidewalk-chalk colors and memories of sweet circus candies onto the floor.

It was glorious.

Bear slept soundly next to the warm oven, a dusting of flour powdered his side.

Gentle birdsong drew her eyes toward the bakery shop's exterior. Morning light filtered through the tall front windows and filled the space with golden warmth. She shook the flour from her hair, brushed it from her hands, and walked into the front where she was welcomed by the abundant sight.

Apothecary jars stuffed to bursting with fat gooey cookies sat atop the large glass case revealing a treasure chest of sugary delights. Twelve delicate French Patisseries, Mille Feuille, invited the eye with a seductive wink. The three layers of flaky puff pastry stuffed with fresh raspberries and rich custard, sat next to a dozen fruit tarts glistening with apricot jam on a toasted, delicate crust. But it was the cupcakes that took her breath away. Two long shelves filled with eight dozen cupcakes, each more luxurious than the next. Seductive and alluring, they called to the viewer from behind sparkling glass with promises of sweet caresses and fulfilled longings. Lorelei shook her head in slight embarrassment. *Was that me? Must have been quite a night,* she wondered in awe.

Each cupcake was topped with unique artful icing that no master could reproduce, no matter haw many attempts were made. Some were mounted in soft sugary peaks, piped with seductive swirls of lemon curd and rosewater. Others stood more majestically. Whipped meringues highlighted by slightly seared tips blanketing decadent red velvet luxury hidden below their alluring caresses, daring the viewer to tip her tongue into the soft folds of egg white and sugar. Another dozen were delicately topped with downy green shadows of fern scented glades, soft and inviting in their call, voluptuous and thrilling to answer.

Each dozen were displayed behind a small brass card holder proudly announcing flavor combinations unheard of in Cobweb Corners—until this morning. Sea Salted Caramel and Cashew dripped golden syrup from gentle white peaks and competed with the Madagascar Vanilla and Honey, which sat on the shelf next to them. The Cinnamon Chocolate Swirl exploded in red-hot hues when compared to the calming Basil Lime cupcakes beside them. Below, Chocolate Cherry

Cordial dripped obscenely onto white enamel trays while the Cardamom Rose, and Lychee cupcakes invited the palate to rest a while with promises of flower-scented paths, before indulging in another coquettish, rose-perfumed kiss.

And sitting alone on the counter, under an ornate glass dome, sat a plate of large pale yellow crumbs, the size of robin's eggs.

A slight knock made her look up at the door.

"Are you open?" the woman asked.

With a smile as wide as the ocean itself, Lorelei answered proudly, "Yes Ma'am, I am. I'm open. Please come in."

Sunlight flooded her small corner of New Hampshire and reflected in her bright, knowing eyes.

Chapter 9

"I was on my way up to the old lighthouse, and I saw your door open. The wildflowers up there this time of year are something to behold," she revealed politely. "This place looks beautiful, just beautiful." And the shy woman held her fingertips to her lips as she gazed over the freshly washed wallpaper. Striped with faded baby's breath bouquets, soft violet and cream tones complimented the tiny floral print giving the little bakery a restored vintage charm. Her eyes rested upon the display case in front of her. "I feel like I've stepped back in time," she said in wonder. "Everything looks so delightful. It's just remarkable, absolutely lovely—"

Lorelei smiled. It was just what she wanted to hear. She looked at this slight and quiet woman, her first customer. She looked like she could be anywhere between forty-five and seventy. Slightly hunched shoulders, and though her hair may have once been auburn, it had faded into a dull brown streaked with grey hairs, but what Lorelei noticed most were the woman's fingers. Thin, delicate, and slightly wrinkled, they looked as though pretzel sticks replaced the bones, and they shook slightly.

"Ma'am, I've been baking all night and I'm just opening up, so forgive me if I look out of sorts," she tried to sound professional, but quickly realized she was still in Adelaide's old bathrobe and apron. She ducked behind the counter and hoped the woman with sweet longing in her eyes didn't notice.

"I haven't made any coffee yet, but if you give me a minute, I'll get pot brewing right away," and she began the first of her new morning ritual—three pots of dark-roasted coffee, loving the rich fuggy aroma rising from the grounds in her hands.

"Paris," the woman said.

"I'm sorry?"

"Paris," she repeated, and Lorelei noticed a wistful note in her voice. "Your cupcakes. Just looking at them, I feel like I'm in a cafe in Paris. It takes my breath away." Her shaky fingertips brushed against her cheek, and Lorelei saw a faded spark lost somewhere in the woman's eyes.

"Really? Paris? Thanks! Never thought of that before, but it sure sounds good. Must be beautiful. Were you there recently?"

The woman became slightly embarrassed. "What? Me? No. No. Never. Just books and movies. But," she paused slightly as though revealing a secret. "I love Paris."

"Why don't you go?" she added with encouragement. "It's just across the ocean, practically a block away when you think about it."

Both women laughed.

"Paris? Me? No, no, no, too far away. Too much to do I guess." She held out her hand, delicate as a tiny bird's wing. "I'm Victoria," she said. "I teach, well, I taught at the elementary school. Retired last May. Friends call me Tori. You should too."

"Tori. That's beautiful. I'm Lorelei. Friends call me Lala. What can I get you?"

Tori's eyes lit up. "Lala? Really? Why that's wonderful! What a special name. I had a girl named Sunshine one year, pretty child too! Eyes as blue as the ocean. But never had a Lala. So many children, so many names. In thirty years of Cobweb Corners' children, I never had a Lala before."

"Oh, it's an odd nickname, I know," Lala replied. "Makes people smile when they say it. I like that. My mama always told me a good name should make people happy." She grabbed a small bakery box and began to fold it. The scent of freshly brewed coffee wafted through the bakery. "Are you looking for anything in particular?"

"Me? Oh no, no— So many beautiful things here. It's nearly impossible to choose," and she continued to caress the cupcakes with her eyes. "But then, I guess that's always been a problem for me." She gave a slight chuckle and drummed her spindly fingertips against her cheek.

"Ma'am?"

"Oh, you know. Choosing things. Making a choice," she explained as she walked back and forth in front of the display case's riches. "I was never any good at it. And one day it seems I looked up, and here I am retired, with a house full of African violets. I'll bring you one. Pretty little things." And she paused. "Like your cupcakes. Delicate and fine. So many colors, it's impossible to pick a favorite."

Lorelei ... a soft morning breeze whispered through the door and she smiled warmly, feeling like she finally arrived. A life of her own.

"Here, this will help." Lorelei gently lifted the ornate glass dome from the plate of yellow sponge cake crumbs.

Lala ...

"Take a bite. Sometimes tasting just a plain bit of my plain sponge cake can help people decide. Only thing is, you need to close your eyes and tell me what it tastes like, okay?"

Tori's smile grew large, as though this free offering of Lala's sponge crumb was as exciting as the Eiffel Tower itself. She reached her delicate hand onto the chipped Blue Willow plate and gently chose a soft morsel of plain yellow sponge. With a childish smile, she closed her eyes and popped it into her small mouth.

"Well?" Lorelei encouraged. "How does that taste? What's it remind you of?"

As Tori delicately chewed the soft sponge, her thin lips grew into a soft smile and her closed eyes relaxed around the edges. Creases disappeared, and for a moment, she was a young girl again. Lala recognized the look. It happened to all of her deserving customers in Kentucky and she was happy it followed her to her new home. Lala took a mental snapshot, for she knew that, once again, she was seeing the face of absolute contentment.

"Oh my word," Tori whispered through a mouthful of delicate sponge cake. "That is the most precious cake—" She thought a moment. "Custard? Is that custard?" She put her hands onto the counter and spread her fingers wide, lost in the creamy rich flavors of eggy curd hinted with a gentle snap of bright lemon. She plopped the last small bite into her gentle mouth and closed her lips slowly. "Birthday? No— birthday cake candles? Can that be?" Embarrassed by her odd declaration, she swallowed the last bit and shyly opened her eyes. "Birthday candles!" She laughed. "Did you ever hear of such a thing? Who ever tasted birthday candles? Don't know where that came from."

Lorelei smiled broadly. It was about to begin. "Ma'am, if you tasted custard and birthday candles in my cake, I'm happy for it. So, with that in mind, can I make a recommendation?" she said with a hint of enticement.

Entranced, Tori smiled but stayed quiet.

"Let me pack up two of these," Lala said and she placed two soft green cupcakes into a small bakery box. "This morning, I'm recommending two Basil-Lime cupcakes. They're bright, slightly herbal, and layered with a cool, creamy lime curd. People tell me the cupcakes taste like their childhood, isn't that pretty? Eat one tonight with a cup of tea, okay? They ought to do the trick. Plus, I want to give you a gift," she added, "seeing that you're my first customer." Lala lifted a delicate French pastry. "It's called a *Mille Feuille*," and she held it above the counter on a thin silver serving knife. Both women peered into the layered pastry as though they were looking into a crystal ball.

Tori's face lit up with a grin wider than the sea outside the door. "Oh my goodness. I can't let you do that! Such a beautiful thing. I just couldn't."

Lala explained in a gentle whisper, "It's a French pastry and I know you'll love it. See?" She guided Tori's eyes to the side of the pastry. "Three layers of golden puff pastry, and in between? Fresh raspberries and my special *creme patissiere*."

"Creme—?"

"Patissiere. It's a French egg custard, a dash of lemon and a little vanilla too," she explained holding the fragile pastry aloft so they both could admire its romantic height and indulgent promises.

"It's too beautiful to eat!" Tori exclaimed.

"Not half as beautiful as the woman eating it," Lala said,

smiling.

Tori radiated and seemed to stand a bit taller as she watched Lala place the exotic pastry in the simple box, gently nudging in next to the soft fern-toned cupcakes.

"That's five dollars even," she said as she handed the box across the old oak counter into Tori's fragile hands.

"Beautiful, just a work of art!" Tori thanked her, paid and was nearly out the door when Lorelei stopped her.

"Tori, one more thing," she asked. "Can I ask you a question? That old lighthouse on the beach. What's the story? Is it open? It looks incredible."

"What? That old place? No dear. It's been abandoned forever. Looks beautiful though. There's a nice trail around it. Wildflowers are beautiful up there. Take a walk around it sometime. I'll be back, Lala." And waving over her shoulder, she was out the door.

Quickly, Lorelei changed into a fresh pair of bell-bottomed jeans—another second hand store find—and though they may have been out of date, they fit her perfectly. She tossed on a crisp linen shirt trimmed with bright embroidered flowers—another yard sale find—and began her first day in the shop. All afternoon she waited on locals who were curious to see the old place come alive again. The house seemed to stand a bit straighter as she was greeted with welcoming smiles and wide-eyed questions about each marvelous, miniature cake. She stood proudly as they marveled at her sugared artistry.

Each new patron was given a bit of her plain Victoria sponge to sample. Jeff Mills smiled as he tasted ocean waves. Grace Ogden said it tasted like roses and her mother's perfume. And old Dorothea Rediker tilted her head back and laughed heartily as she tasted a memory so sweet it brought tears to her eyes. Each left with a checkered cardboard box filled with luxurious treats and, more importantly, Lorelei's prescribed cupcake tucked in among her freshly baked treats.

By four o'clock, thrilled with plump sales and diminishing stock, she flipped over the old sign on the front door. *Closed.*

Come back soon! it read in fancy faded script. A whimsical painted spider dangled in the large O. She looked at Bear who sat on the sunny porch outside, thumping his tail to an unheard beat against the sun bleached boards and called, "Hey Bear! How about we go for a walk?" Wiping her hands on her apron, she balled it up, tossed it behind the counter.

The walk up the beach revived her. She looked back upon her new home rising like a twisted asparagus sprout from the dunes and she laughed. Misshapen and mysterious with an alluring fairy-tale charm, it was the perfect fit for her new life.

Ahead, the tall lighthouse beckoned her. It towered over the few stunted pines and its mystique was too entrancing to ignore.

"C'mon, Bear! Time to explore the new neighborhood."

The lighthouse sat upon a small, rocky bluff, rising over the beach. What was once a cedar railing, now broken and rotting in the sand, guided the traveller up craggy stone steps, and like a perversely abandoned yellow brick road, it led the young woman and dog to the base of the massive structure. Weeds sprouted freely, and what may turn to goldenrod in late summer, formed a rough hewn hedge between sand and path.

The lighthouse door was a marvel of ancient oak and brass. Set firmly in the stone base, it looked as if it led to Narnia's winter forest.

She leaned her back against the cool stone and tilting her head back as far as possible, she looked up, up, up. At the very top was a circular iron deck that twisted around the entire narrow pinnacle of the lighthouse.

Bet you could see all the way to Paris from up there ... she thought, and a wry smile crept onto her lips.

I wonder ...

She began to explore the large base, firmly rooted deep into the earth. The majestic structure stood tall and proud as she trailed her hand along the whitewash and sauntered toward the rear of the lighthouse. A smile crept upon her lips when she saw the attached stone structure, a keeper's quarters shaded by stunted pines and graceful hemlock. One story tall, it appeared sunken in the earth, the size of a large room with a massive chimney rising from the back wall.

Windows were boarded up with haphazard plywood and aging beams, rot dripping like molasses. A fluorescent orange sign, hanging by one remaining staple, screamed *No Trespassing*.

Its silence was absurd.

Bear followed closely behind, sniffing at the damp and weedy edges as Lorelei explored the old structure.

She walked to a large door, metal-plated and imposing, grown green with spotty lichen and patina's age marks. Though a hefty lock shouted an impossible entrance, she shook the door handle anyway. She rattled the lock and the door held firm. She became more curious about the abandoned landmark and continued to the rear of the decaying building. Hidden from the sun, the canopy of evergreens created a dank, cool space. The weeds grew abundantly in the shade and cooled the ocean air considerably. A warped, plywood board hung from the rear window, breaking the monotony of the old stone wall. The bottom corner obscenely torqued with seasons of salty damp air; it begged to be inspected.

Curious, she lifted the board whose protective qualities were lost with age, and it twanged mightily beneath her finger tips.

Loose!

A chill ran over her frame and she saw the potential to explore the inside.

"I'm just gonna peek inside, that's all Bear," she told the patient mutt at her side. Lifting the rotting corner was easier than expected. The warped board torqued so heavily that it pulled the nails from the old casement seasons ago and the entire bottom sprang free in her hands.

She quickly looked around, making sure she wasn't being observed. The building was abandoned for goodness sake. *It's not like I'm a thief!* she justified. *Just going to take a look, that's all.*

Lifting the plywood away like an old garage door, she propped it open with a pine branch and peered inside.

Dappled greenish light sifted into the abandoned room and she gazed with wonder. The entire room sat well below ground level, at least an eight foot drop. To the left, a large stone staircase dropped from the outer door into the room.

Must have been incredibly romantic in its day, but now? Age and isolation took its toll. A rotting sofa sat in the center of the room and had sprung a few holes. Rusted springs and cotton batting exploded from its cushions. Like wild mushrooms, they grew grey and mysterious in the fecund space.

A chair lay on its side, toppled by some unseen hand years back, a dusty flagstone floor, and when she saw the opposite wall, her eyes sparkled with curiosity. Standing floor to ceiling, from wall to wall, a bookcase overflowed with swollen books. Absorbing dampness and moisture, the sponges of ancient words called to her for a closer look.

The drop from the window sill was intimidating. Taking a deep breath, she decided to let curiosity win and she swung her limber legs over the sill.

"Bear. You wait here boy, and don't tell nobody."

The hound thumped his weighty tail against cool earth, and watched patiently.

Her Kentucky tree climbing days quickly returned to her as she grabbed the sill to her right and deftly spun her hips around, dropping down against the wall with a mighty humph.

A swift intake of air and she dropped to the floor below, landing firmly upon two trusty Keds.

The dust rose in a cloud around her feet and the air was instantly cooler in this shadowy space, smelling of ash and must. Crouching, she looked at the massive fireplace to her side. Black charcoaled logs, half-burned, half-lived, their charred tips worn down like fat dull pencils sunken in a mound of grey ash.

Brushing the fall from her jeans, she tiptoed to the bookcase and gazed at the stained leather spines. Ornately trimmed with leathery tones of reds, golds, and umbers, they revealed their contents slowly. Brushing her fingertips along the spines, she read old titles like *The Night Sky, Stars Over Monadnock, A Book of Wonders, A Child's Guide to the Stars*. Other titles were worn away, obliterated with age and mildew.

Outside, Bear gave a few concerned throaty grumbles.

"It's okay boy!" she hollered. "No worries."

Her eyes became accustomed to the diminished light and she noticed the far wall was a massive convex curve and held an ornate wooden door.

The lighthouse!

Decoratively scrolled hinges and a tarnished handle gave the massive oaken door a significance that was incongruous with the rest of the room. She twisted the handle and it held firm, locked tight.

"Damn," she muttered.

A concerned bark from above answered her.

"Bear, it's okay, I'm coming out," she yelled toward the upper window. The sun was setting and the light was fading more rapidly than she expected.

That's when she noticed the window's height.

"Uh oh," she mumbled.

The window was too far above her, out of her reach.

"Oh damn ... Oh damn!"

In her curiosity to explore the hidden room, she neglected to plan an escape route. There was no way to jump that high and both doors were locked firmly.

Another anxious bark from above.

And another.

Her heart froze when she heard the deep voice from above.

"Bear? Is that you?" called the kind male voice. "What are you doing out here alone boy?"

Chase!

Lorelei instantly panicked. *Oh God no! Not again!*

Like a hunted mouse, she scurried her eyes across the room looking for a place to hide and found nothing. No options, no chance, no way. She was caught. Dejected, she threw herself heavily on the couch, which instantly gave way under her and, collapsing in a loud crash, topped over on its back, sending a cloud of dust through the air.

"What the hell?" the disembodied voice yelled from above.

"Aw damn," she mumbled. Knowing she lost, Lorelei lay flat on her back waiting for the inevitable. She looked up at the ceiling rafters, her legs dangling above, brightly capped by two small, white sneakers. She swayed them gently to an unheard melody and they fluttered like two doves rising from the town dump.

A flashlight swept through the room and like a spotlight,

landed upon her twiggy legs suspended in the dusty air.

That's when she heard the hearty guffaw. "Oh no—"

She heard his rich baritone laughter echo through the stone chamber and she decided to take a risk. Holding one leg straight and firm, she waved her foot in a cheerful hello.

He lost it. His chest convulsed as rich bursts of laughter rose from his lungs and showered the room below. "Oh my God, stop," he howled. "I can't, I can't—" And as laughter choked his throat, he was unable to finish the sentence.

Lorelei lay below and listened to his laughter. Embarrassed, mortified even, she flipped over on her side and chose to fess up. Kneeling on the couch's back upon the floor, she lifted her head up and proudly exclaimed the obvious.

"Hi, Chase! Me again!" And she waved brightly.

He smiled broadly at the sight. A small woman climbing over a filthy couch, waving in the dusk as though she were in a ball gown.

"Miss Lorelei," he called down in mock surprise. "Come here often?"

"Oh sure," she said, attempting a sophisticated flip of her hair. "The food is wonderful, but the atmosphere could use a little help." Cross-eyed, she picked a stray twig from her hair.

"But tonight? The entertainment is outstanding," he said as a wide smile spread across his face.

Busted, she rested her arms on the couch's edge and peered up at him. "Well, I try! Show is sold out tonight. Tough luck kiddo! Try tomorrow. I'll be appearing in the frozen food aisle at the supermarket."

"See ya there! After midnight I assume?" He moved away from the window and hollered over his shoulder. "I guess I'll try then. See ya!"

"No! Chase. I'm teasing. Wait. Please?"

His face reappeared, infused with a gentle smirk.

"Well? You gonna help me?" she asked.

"Lady, that's going to require some back up. I'm going to need major reinforcement for this. Rescue squad. Fire trucks, maybe even the entire police force. In fact. I may have to call the White House on this one."

He was enjoying the show too much, and she knew it. As

she looked up at his face, so handsome and warm, she held his eyes a moment and felt her core warm in the glow his smile.

She smiled up at him. "A big officer like you? Sure you can't do this on your own?"

He dangled a key chain in the window.

"Well, I've got the keys right here. Trouble is, breaking and entering is against the law, and I'm not sure what I should do. Seems like you have a habit of climbing in people's windows. You may have to spend the night."

"Chase! No, don't. I can explain!" She stood and pleaded with his brown eyes.

Bear jumped up and rested his mighty paws on the ledge and gave a few concerned barks.

He spoke to the hound like a crime-solving partner. "Now, how many crooks do you know who wear white Keds?" He looked down at the young woman in dusty ruins. "Seems to me we have to get you some major steel-toed shoes so you can just kick the door down. What do you think? Maybe Sophie has a pair she's not using?"

"Hey! That's not fair."

"No, what's not fair is breaking into my grandfather's lighthouse. That's not fair."

Things were getting serious and for the first time, Lorelei felt she had crossed over a dangerous line.

"Your grandfather's?" She took a deep breath. "Chase, I'm sorry. Really. I just wanted to see inside. The window was wide open! Sort of. I'm not hurting anything and no one was around so— The lighthouse looked so cool and— I'm sorry. Please help me."

He gave her a brief scolding glance with an additional cup of authority and left the window.

"Chase!" she hollered.

Relieved, she heard his keys rattling in the old door's lock and it swung open upon rusty hinges.

"Miss Bradley, we have to do something about this," he said leaning against the doorway. "This is breaking and entering, and this time you don't own the deed to the place. I do."

"I'm sorry," she said sincerely. She tried to ignore the warmth of his smiling lips and eyes that offered even more. "I know, I know. It's wrong. I was taking Bear for a walk and I just wanted to explore. Really! I'm not even sure how—"

"You can explore from outside. This place is old, Lorelei. The roof is rotting and who knows what could happen. You could have been trapped in here." She noticed a concern had crept into his voice.

Bear wandered into the doorway and gave a few throaty sniffs in the air.

"Well yes, I guess, but when I saw the books, I had to see. You know? They looked so old and I guess—"

"You guess what?"

"I wanted to see what books they were. And—" She knew her excuse was failing in his eyes and she folded her arms against her chest.

"The books," he said. "That's all you were interested in? Seeing the books?" He sounded doubtful.

"Well. That and—"

"Yes?"

"The lighthouse." She gave in and confronted him under the lids of downcast eyes. His imposing figure framed the doorway as he gently tossed the keys in his hands.

They stared at each other, and without purpose or thought, slowly, they acknowledged that it was something richer. It rose in the air and surrounded them in its subtle warm glow. It was remarkable, and as it grew, they became aware.

Aware of each other.

Aware of their own accelerated heartbeats, perfectly tuned to a matching rhythm.

The keys stopped jingling and silence settled upon them.

And then?

They both smiled, acknowledging the shared moment between them, and she held the sweet scent in her lungs. Empty for too long, she finally understood why so many people wrote about love in a language too soft to speak.

"The lighthouse, huh?" he questioned softly.

"The lighthouse," she responded.

"Let's go then."

Her face lit up. "Really?"

"I give in. You get the grand tour," he told her. "But the dog stays below."

"Sure! Sure thing. He'll be fine," she said.

Chase walked to the large oaken door and selecting a key from his abundant ring, unlocked the lighthouse door. With a hint of pride glowing across his face, he gave it a hard tug and swung it wide open.

Chapter 10

Awestruck, Lorelei glided inside. She knew the air already; it smelled like her childhood. Lost, decayed, and saturated with abandoned hopes, it made her shiver. But there was something else here too. Just below the surface, she could hear the hidden potential like an infant's heartbeat, a blooming unfurling beneath her feet.

Maybe it was the building.

Maybe it was the adventure ahead.

Or perhaps it was the man at her side.

She smiled at him and took a few steps around the circular base.

A cool greenish light resided in the secret space, ineffectively dappling the room from tall, arched windows that spiraled up the conical tower. She felt like she was in a sacred room. A church or synagogue-like silence pervaded the air and demanded respect.

He flicked a switch and Lorelei's eyes grew wide with wonder and awe. A few bare light bulbs hung like naked birds and guided her eyes up the concentric iron staircase that spun around and around to a dizzying height. Though paint was peeling and cobwebs hung like ancient hair, Cinderella's castle never looked more romantic.

"Oh my goodness," she said in awe. "I feel so small."

"You ready?" he asked.

"Really?" Excitement exploded from her throat as her eyes followed the iron railing, spinning in diminishing concentric spirals up to the top where it was lost in the dark.

"Really." He smiled. "The stairs look rickety, but they're

solid. Hold onto the railing, and if heights are a problem—"

He never finished the sentence. Lorelei had begun the climb and within seconds, was already a full spiral above him.

"Chase! This is amazing!"

Zing... zing ... zing the echo replied.

Holding the railing, she looked down at him and their eyes met. She smiled broadly. Hair hanging freely, standing in the abandoned tower, she was the image of absolute contentment.

Rapunzel could save the prince, even without magical ropes of hair. A simple glance was all it took.

"Well? You coming up too?" she teased.

Even Goldilocks got to choose her own bed.

She held his eyes a long time. Chase took a deep breath. Not because of the climb ahead of him, but because of what he was climbing toward.

"You want the guided tour? Or are you just going to fly up to the roof on your own?" And then he mumbled, "Wouldn't surprise me if you sprouted wings." He watched her practically dance up the spiral stairs. "The door to the parapet is locked, but somehow, I don't think that'll stop you."

With a slight puppy grin, she said, "Chase, I'm sorry. Really. This is all so new. I just couldn't— I've never even saw the ocean before I moved here! And a lighthouse? Wow!"

Oww oww oww came the echo.

Her eyes flew through the space like she was searching for the echo. She followed each swirl and curve of the plaster covered walls, thick as buttercream on a forgotten wedding cake, and discovered colors she had never recognized as beautiful.

Until now.

"It's all too much. So—well." She let out a relieved sigh. "Thanks. Thank you—yes. A guided tour would be lovely."

His smile was all she needed. Chase climbed the steps toward her and began.

"The Cobweb Corners lighthouse was built in 1872 and operated for about seventy years." He sounded as though he had said this a million times before. "It's one hundred and fifty-six feet tall and contains two hundred, fourteen steps, and at your rate, you'll probably fly past half of them. My grandfather bought it in—"

"This view!" Lorelei reached the first window and looked out over the ocean. She rubbed her fist against the dirty glass and pressing her face against the window, peered through.

"Lala, that's nothing," he said. "Wait until the top."

She smiled at him, a smudge of dirt on her cheek, a slight question on her lips.

"What?" He asked.

"My name," she said with a small laugh shaking her head.

"What? Lala?"

She looked at him and chuckled a little. "Lala. You still don't have it."

"What?"

"My name," she explained with a kind laugh. "You say Lala so seriously, like its a brand of cement mix or something. Too heavy. Make it more of a song. Why so heavy, Chase?"

She saw she hit a nerve. She tilted her head a bit, waiting, hoping he'd explain.

He didn't.

"So?" She saw he retreated a bit beneath his brow and she changed the subject. "Your granddaddy …?"

"Yes!" He was relieved. "He bought the lighthouse at a public auction in the 50s. Paid a hefty sum for it, too. He planned on turning it into a cafe or something. But never did. The National Park Service and The New England Society for Historic Preservation are really interested in it. I haven't made up my mind to sell yet. Maybe I should."

The pair continued the climb up the decorative iron grate steps, Chase talking, Lorelei listening. Climbing in tandem, they reached that rhythm that only potential lovers recognize, and the unspoken words warmed them both.

Without warning, fanfare, or formal declaration, Lorelei rose from the staircase hatchway into the upper lantern room. The sound of the waves echoed in the magical space and late afternoon sun flooded through tall, glass walls surrounding her, filling the space with a rosy glow. Above her, the copper cupola arched toward the sky in an ancient web of iron beams and dark, hidden recesses.

And in the center was a massive idol of glass.

Godly.

Perched upon a cast iron altar, a monstrous conglomeration of weighty prismed glass, copper sheathing, and cast iron holsters. The light itself.

It was marvelous.

"My lord," she exclaimed, "it's like something from a sci-fi movie!"

"Yes," he said, "It's *Dr. Strangelove* meets *Alien*." His warm laughter filled her. "It's an oldie, and died decades ago. It's beautiful, though, isn't it?"

She looked at him. His pride was so endearing. His connection to the past, and his appreciation for the history glowed from his core. She let it fill her and as she held it in her lungs, she wondered, is it this magical space? Is that why my heart is beating and my chest is tight? Or is it this man?

Lorelei …

She quickly turned her gaze to the windows that separated her from the wind.

Lala… it sang.

"Chase? Can we—"

"Walk around the gallery?" he answered.

Loreeeeelieeeee … The call was insistent.

"Quickly, yes. I'd love that."

When he unlocked the ornate door, Lorelei felt the fresh wind swirl through the lighthouse, and like a small tornado, it curled through the magical space and was soon lost in the domed cupola over her head.

With the grace of a mermaid, she glided onto the windy gallery, a five-foot-wide balcony circling the lighthouse's top story.

Chase watched as without a care, without fear or apprehension, Lorelei stepped to the railing and held on to the black cast iron rail. She held firmly. But not for fear of falling or being blown over.

No.

She held on because for the first time in her life, her heart was so full that she feared the wind might find her undiscovered wings and she'd fly straight up into the firmament slowly revealing her wonders to the world.

Lorelieeeeeee ...

Keeping her eyes closed, she tilted her head back and let the wind caress her hair, her face, her neck. It found the secret spaces in her chest, the creases of her arms, her thighs. The wind blew across her light embroidered blouse and circled around her wrists, kissing the soft skin below her palm, and teasing the colorful flowers upon her sleeves and cuffs.

It was about to begin. She could feel it.

She closed her eyes and succumbed to the wind.

One by one, each magically sown flower, each silken petal and linen stamen released themselves from their embroidered prison of lace and cotton and without gravity's objection, flew gracefully in the air around her. Multiplying in number, dividing and doubling, dancing through the magical air, each flower gently exploded into a hundred more and Lorelei was in the center of it all. Lost in a blizzard of flowers, she laughed cheerfully.

Chase watched, awestruck.

"What the—"

She stood so beautifully, serene and whole as flower petals rose from her sleeves and gently flew up into the stratosphere, multiplied by dozens of blooms rising magically from her hair. The flowers fell back upon her, a shower of confetti made from petals and blooms.

And she simply stood there, as if this was an average day, an angel among a shower of flowers.

"Lorelei—?"

"Beautiful!" She cried into the sky. "It's so beautiful. Air and wind. This is incredible," she called out to the wind with gratitude and grace. Chase saw tears running down her face.

"Baby?"

She stood among a soft drift of flowers that hid her feet from view. The receding wind blew them around her ankles and they gently cascaded over the edge where they swirled into the evening air. She turned to look at him, and her smile revealed a woman in possession of her spirit and thankful for the new life surrounding her.

"I found it, Chase," she said, starlight in her eyes.

"Found it?"

"Home. I'm home."

"Lorelei," he paused. "Your sleeves."

She looked down at her arms and noticed the tattered cuffs. Where embroidered flowers and vines used to circle the trim, all that remained were a few colorful threads hanging like abandoned feathers, moving softly in the diminishing wind.

"Oh." She looked at his eyes and smiled serenely. "Chase," she said quietly, "can we sit down? We should have a talk."

A beautiful light grew upon her face and she invited him in.

Two miles away, in a gas station on the edge of town, Jeff Mills opened up the bakery parcel he bought that afternoon. Kooky baker, but she seemed nice. Even gave him a free cupcake.

He held the gift in his grease-stained hand. Its delicate artistry a sharp contrast to the repair garage surrounding him.

What did she say?

Something about how memories taste. Weird chick.

But if the cupcake in his hand was anything like the sweet morsel of sponge cake he tried, he was going to be in heaven. What was it about her?

Odd though. Ocean? Why did he say he tasted the ocean? In a piece of plain yellow cake?

Blue frosting whirled over the cupcake in his hand, like a robin's egg in a giant's paw, and without even peeling back the paper wrapper, he took a massive bite.

Salty waves and fleeting air filled his memories. Speed and joy—powerful balance as sturdy feet gripped a wet board under him and without warning or thought, he threw his head back and laughed aloud. Full and hard, mouth full of blue salty icing, delicate sponge filling his cheeks, his laughter echoed through the cool garage and it felt good.

Damn good.

"Damn!" he yelled, and dove in for another greedy mouthful. Eyes wide, he licked the frosting from the corners of his mouth, hungry for more.

Eyes searching, he spotted his old surf board in the corner.

Hidden by tires, tools, and old, stained oil drums, its top edge was barely visible, covered in a decade of dust and grease.

"Hey," he whispered, as though talking to an old friend.

He sat still a long time.

Later that night, if you listened closely, you could hear the laughter of a forty-five-year-old garage mechanic rediscovering the joy he gave up when adulthood called. His bare feet clenched the wet and waxy board under him and he released himself to the joy of the waves. Surfing at night, surrounded by starlight and unbridled joy, Jeff found himself finally free.

Across town, Grace Ogden sat at her kitchen window and ate a delicate bite of the pink and violet cupcake the new baker had so graciously given to her. For free even! Odd young lady, but she was kind, Grace thought.

What was it about her?

As the sponge filled her mouth, she swore that roses were blooming … in her lungs? Couldn't be. She nearly choked the scent was so powerful. She smiled at a distant memory.

Mama?

Another bite.

And another smile.

She tapped her fork against the delicate plate a few times.

Another breath of rose petals filled her heart and bloomed throughout the kitchen.

"Mama's roses—"

Brushing off her knees, she decided to get to work. Mama's roses were neglected for far too long. What was she thinking? For twenty years they lie in wait under a bed of rotting leaves and weeds as tall as corn. She simply had to get to work!

"Grace? You okay?" her neighbor called. Grace never worked on the house and was rarely outside. Ever.

"Fine! I'm fine Judy!" she called back cheerily. "Decided to see if I can save Mama's roses! They've been ignored for far too long. What was I thinking? Hope there's a chance."

Judy approached her yard. "There's always a chance! You need some help?"

Grace paused. It was unlike her to accept help from anyone.

"Judy," she said welcoming, "I would love a hand."

The two women sank upon their knees, loving the feel of the reawakening earth beneath their fingers.

And in a small apartment across the street from the elementary school, a retired teacher picked up the phone and dialed.

"Cobweb Corners Travel, how can I help?"

"Pepper? It's me Tori."

"Well! Victoria! Nice to hear from you! What can I do for you?"

"Pepper, remember that trip I've been putting off?"

"Paris?" Her voice hinted at a spark of joy.

Through a mouthful of delicious pink sponge, she garbled, "That's the one. Book it!"

On a couch, in a silent room, old Dorothea Rediker fell asleep, dreaming of a trip she and her husband took so many decades ago. Across the country in a train. Making love in the reserved suite they booked with their meager savings—such passion she thought she'd die from happiness.

The old woman smiled beautifully in her sleep, a hint of fragrant frosting haunted her lower lip as her body remembered the love she had felt, the love she had given away, and the love still to come.

For the first time in a long while, peace filled her soul, and she slept soundly that night.

And on a small balcony, suspended a hundred and fifty-six feet above the calming ocean and lit by a clear twilight sky, two strangers fell in love. They fell simply and without complications. One spoke softly of his loss and heartbreak.

Watching the love of his life fade away as the metered drip of the IV put her to sleep for yet another silent night.

The other spoke of a lonely life in a dirty trailer deep in the Kentucky hills, her alcoholic father and the magical aunt who saved her.

They listened as the other's stories took unexpected turns and revealed hidden delights. Fran's desire for Chase to find love filled Lorelei with a compassion she had never known before, and Chase wondered how the small woman at his side found her strength. He fell in love with her radiant joy.

"But Lorelei, the flowers," he whispered. "I saw them. They— they floated away and—"

"Chase," she said, as though she were talking to a frightened kid, "that stuff happens. Always has. I decided long ago it was more fun to live with it than to figure it out. It's simple."

She gazed into the distant firmament, her eyes searching for the stars and their lovely secrets.

"But—"

"Nope," she said with a voice of poetic insight. "There are no buts. Like I told you, Aunt Adelaide knew and she tried to teach me, but I was so young. 'Listen to that wind,' she'd say, like it was a song or something." She looked directly at him. "That's how I get my recipes. The wind. It's always there, kinda like an angel I guess. All my life. Kids thought I was weird. And the supermarket? Where I used to work?" She shook her head and laughed a little. "They thought I was nuts! Baking flavors they never even heard of. Poor folks, come to think of it. With all the flavors out there? Who wouldn't want a taste of everything? Not in Bentfork, that's for sure."

She paused a moment. "I know my mama knew. Scared her though. She used to look at me funny when I was playing outside. Wind in my hair, messing it all up. By then the booze destroyed her. Blocked her all up. And my Daddy? Who knows. He was just so angry he couldn't ever let any light in. Ever."

"No other family around?"

She found a star deep in the distance and made a silent wish.

"Nope," she said, hugging her knees tightly. "Just me and

Bear." She buried Beeker deep into the tightly locked cement box she stored below her heart. It was getting easier and easier to forget that chapter.

Just turn the page. Erase, cross out, and move on. Right?

Even Rapunzel kept a secret high in her tower. She had to.

Lorelei looked into his deep eyes, warm, trusting, and inviting.

"Chase," she said, "I've never been in love. I've never had a real boyfriend, and I don't have much except an old hound, an old gingerbread house that might tip over any day, even the clothes I wear have other people's memories embedded in every stitch. I don't know how to do any of this," she told him simply. "But what I'm feeling right now? When I look at you?" She reached out and took his hand. "I think Fran was right. I think my aunt was right." She took a breath and looked into the sky for the words. "I'm glad you saw the flowers. That's me. It's who I am. And right now? I'm going to ask you to kiss me, flowers and all."

Chase laughed. Loud and hard and it felt good. The joy in his lungs filled him and overflowed onto the balcony floor and drifted up into the twilight air.

"Lorelei," he said in wonder. "Who are you?" He searched her shining face for answers and saw magical, starlit eyes looking back. He whispered, "Where did you come from?" He reached out and stroked her dazzling cheek with his hand.

"The wind," she responded with ease and a gentle shrug. "The wind brought me here." With wonder in her voice she told him, "I've got more flowers in store—trouble is, I can't control it."

She leaned forward, taking his rugged face in her soft palms and pressed her lips, soft as velvet against his. She wasn't surprised to feel his tears against her palm. She knew he had traveled a long distance to reach this place, and she gave herself freely.

When their souls met high above the ground, both knew it was a reunion of hearts, centuries in the making and seconds to fulfill. Breath mingled with breath and heartbeats found their symbiotic rhythm. As joy flooded through their cores upon recognition of this unintended meeting, their muscles tightened and relaxed and they found themselves discovering the other self they had lost, a rhythm they had forgotten— until now. Pressing chest to chest, lips soft and yielding to the other, they found themselves slowly entwining hands, outstretched like vines clinging to limbs, the needed support in a wind too strong to bear alone, and they faced the elements together.

Far below, flying across the ocean waves on a sleek and faded surfboard, a middle-aged man howled in joyful recognition as well. He sped across the surface and his voice carried up, up, up, and landed upon the hearts of the lovers who, finding recognition in the other's eyes, knew they would no longer live in the darkened world they knew before.

And peaceful lovers all across the town bedded down for another night in their small corner of Cobweb Corners, New Hampshire.

Chapter 11

"No way!" Connor slammed his beer bottle on the wooden bar with a hefty thud. "Dude! No way! And then you—? At the lighthouse? Wait, what?"

Attempting to hide his grin, Chase took a long pull from his beer. He knew his story was too unbelievable to hear, but there it was.

They huddled at the end of the bar. Their conversation punctuated by a few loud guffaws and raised, winking brows. The afternoon crowd was winding down at Thoreau's Pub and only a few patrons remained. Country tunes piped in overhead from an old speaker nailed to a rafter as the bartender lazily washed a few wine glasses, his mind miles away.

"Here, look at this," Chase pulled a small cotton flower from his pocket and placed it gently on the bar. "Here's one of them. There were hundreds. Thousands. All over the place. One was stuck on my ass. It was like a blizzard of crazy flowers! I'm telling you, it was unreal."

The two men stared at the tiny blue blossom, no larger than a dime, its edges frayed like old parchment paper. It sat, an innocuous object, surrounded by two large men who gazed upon the magical blossom like frightened kittens.

They watched it cautiously.

It sat still.

They stared a long time.

"See?" Chase whispered.

Connor tried flicking it with his fork.

"Yo! It's not a snake! It's not going to bite you!" Chase picked up the delicate flower and put it back in his pocket.

"Chase, you watched it rain flowers man!" He leaned in and spoke low, conspiratorially. "What the hell was that?"

"Yeah, I did." Chase took another deep gulp of his cold beer. "I saw her stand on the galley's edge, and that wind? It was no ordinary wind. I swear, I thought she was about to fly away." He picked at the damp label on the bottle distractedly. "But, she just seemed, well, comfortable, you know?"

"Yeah?"

"At the moment, it didn't look weird or anything. It just looked—"

"Uh huh—"

"Well, amazing! And, um, natural, too? I guess? Or unreal. I don't know. It looked so easy. Like she was used to it?" He began to speak more rapidly. "It's impossible, I know. And I know it sounds crazy, but it's what I saw, and I knew—" He stopped suddenly, his eyes miles away.

"And what?"

Chase stared at his friend and his words suddenly failed. Too many images flooded his core and he broke contact. He looked away. He took another long pull from his beer and let it run down his throat in icy rivulets. It was all too much. Fran and the hospital bed, the IV drip all swirled through his recessed memories and became lost, a second seat to something new—a blizzard of magical cotton flowers.

"Chase. You gotta let this out. What is it?"

"I don't know!"

"It's what you saw and—?" Connor encouraged him.

"More beers fellas?" Sophie's cheerful question was overpoweringly loud and both men jumped. She smacked her tray on the counter and shouted, "Hey, Phil! Grab me two more vodka tonics for table seven and another Merlot for the three top." She winked at Chase. "How 'bout it fellas? A refill? The deep fried bacon mac and cheese is real good today."

Chase looked away. "No, Soph. I'm fine."

"Same here. Just the check, thanks," Connor said.

Sophie looked at the two men. Something was up. They sat more rigidly and they were disconnected somehow. Distant.

"You okay?" She looked at them, slightly suspicious.

"Fine! We're fine. Chase," he said turning to his friend, "I got this one. I'll meet you outside."

Relieved, Chase tossed on his jacket and was out the door.

"What was that all about?" she asked.

"Oh, you know Chase." Connor tried to sound unconcerned. "Fran is still a big thing, and dating and all."

"Dating? Who dating? You mean me? The clambake? Did I do something wrong?" She looked toward the door gnawing on her gum as Chase escaped into the parking lot.

"No! No, Sophie you're fine. It's the new girl, Lorelei."

Sophie raised her brows in a subtle pinch.

"Lorelei?" She paused a moment and let the information sink in. "Oh," she said through a slightly clenched jaw. "Got it. Boy do I get it now." She grabbed her cocktail tray and sped away.

"No! Sophie, not like that." But it was too late. She sped past the bar and left the kitchen door swinging angrily in her wake.

"Damn." He tossed a twenty on the bar and ran after his friend outside.

Chase stood at the edge of the lot, hands deep in his pockets and stared off into the distance, his back solid and still as a massive tree trunk.

"Buddy, you okay?"

Chase nodded a bit, shoulders firm, fists clenched deep in his pockets.

"Connor, man, I don't know how you did it." His voice was tight.

Connor stayed in the distance. "Did what?"

"Randy." Chase turned to look at his friend. He knew the subject was painful, but Connor was the only other guy he knew who has experienced a loss as great as his own.

Chase turned away. "I don't know how you got through it." His voice became more distant.

Connor took a deep breath and looked at his friend in the twilight. His dark jacket reflected the yellow neon light from the bar's window, a blinking warning sign silently asking him to proceed with caution.

It was slow at first, almost imperceptible. Then, as Connor watched, Chase began to shake. His friend's shoulders collapse inwardly and jerked with small, subtle, spasms.

"Hey," he tried. But it was ineffective. Inept almost.

"I can't. I can't," he choked. And then the tears began to fall. Chase pulled his large fist from his pocket and grabbed his forehead as if he was trying to squeeze the tears, the rage, the pain back into his head instead of releasing them in a lonely parking lot perched on the edge of the world.

Connor approached him. Tears like this always made him uncomfortable and talking about Randy was even more painful. But when he saw the broken man in front of him and the pain he tried to hold as though it were a badge, he stepped in as naturally as a father approaches a frightened child.

"Chase, you gotta let this stuff out. Really man. Don't hold it in. I tried to and it doesn't work. Believe me. It just makes you sick. Remember? I walled myself away when she died. I drank. Quit going to work. I nearly ruined my life as well."

Chase took a deep breath. Hands back in his trouser pockets, out of sight. Clenched tightly like a rock holding a precious diamond.

"Yeah. I know," he said. "I remember." He looked at Connor by his side. "You stank, too."

Both guys laughed a bit, acknowledging the shared memory, and silently knew more was to come.

"Connor, man. I'm tired." He looked squarely into Connor's eyes. "I really am. I don't think I'm ready for this. For any of it. I'm just spent."

"I'm sure. After the year you went through? What you both went through. No wonder. But Chase. You gotta let this stuff out. It's toxic man. It poisons you."

Chase laughed. "You sound like Keighley." He smiled brightly. "Are we getting all crystals and earth magic hippy dippy stuff now?"

"I guess I do sound like her. But that woman saved me. She's right. And it's not just the marriage. It's what I learned from her too. Ya know?"

Chase filled his lungs with cool night air. "Yeah. I know. You're a lucky man. She's amazing. Really. Not sure I buy all that palm reading stuff though."

"What? Dude! You saw a woman make it rain flowers. You

saw a woman stand on the edge of the galley while she was lost in a snowstorm of flowers, man. And then you rolled around on a lighthouse galley a thousand feet above the ground with those same flowers stuck to your ass and you have a problem with my wife's palm reading? Are you kidding me?"

Chase paused a moment and said, "The lighthouse is actually one hundred, fifty-seven feet above ground, not a thousand."

The two men stared at each other. Easily, and without language, they recognized the implausibility of their lives. Chase broke first. A smile crept across his solid jaw and as it grew, his cheeks swelled a bit, raising the grin into an acknowledgement of the absurdity they both faced.

That was all Connor needed. He broke. A loud guffaw erupted from his mouth and exploded into the night air. Chase followed suit. He lifted his head back and let the laughter rise from his chest and burst into the night. It rose above him and both men found themselves united unexpectedly as they howled and gagged in the parking lot. Clutching their bellies, bent over in abundant release, they emptied their lungs upon the concrete and rising like a wave, stood up and bent backwards filling their lungs with more choking, silvery air and the pattern repeated and repeated until both men were spent.

Chase wiped tears away from his joyfully burning eyes. "Amazing, just amazing."

"How'd we get here? Holy crap, man." A few remaining convulsions shook his chest. "You ever think something like this was possible? I'm married to the most beautiful fortune-teller who ever lived."

"Me? No way. Not a chance. Never saw this coming in a million years." Chase wiped his sleeve across his wet face. "Never. But since Lorelei came to town? Who knows—who knows. Things are changing. Maybe that's a good thing." Chase heaved a sigh and sat heavily on the concrete lot. He leaned against his truck and pulled his knees up almost like a kid.

Gazing into the firmament, he said simply, "She asked me to. You know that? Just before she died. She asked me to."

"Asked you what?" Connor plunked himself down beside Chase.

"Franny. She wanted me to get married. Have a family. The whole thing. She said it." He looked at Connor who's gaze was lost in the vast New England sky above him. He looked so confident. So at ease. Chase wondered if he, too, could ever reach that point.

"Really? She said that?"

"Yeah. And not just once. A lot. Drove me crazy at the time. But now?"

Connor waited. "Now what?" he asked, eyes never shifting from the stars who slowly revealed themselves and their hopeful, distant light.

Chase looked at his friend. "I'm kinda thankful. I know what she meant." It was hard to say.

Connor stayed silent. From his years of friendship with this guy, he knew when to wait. Eventually, Chase would fill in the answers.

"It's scary. Really scary. Ya know?" Chase said.

"Um hum," came a soft reply. "I know."

"It's like I hate going home to that empty house. But at the same time, it's where Fran is."

"Chase, really?"

"It's all dark and quiet. I try leaving lights on so when my night shift is over, the place doesn't look so lonely."

"No, not about that."

"Huh?" Chase was confused.

"Franny."

"What about Franny?"

"She's not there. She wouldn't want you to think that either. You know that. I know that."

"Connor—"

"No. She's not. Why do you think she kept asking you to move on? She doesn't want you be alone. She told you man. You were lucky. You got conversations I never had a chance to."

"Connor—"

"No. Really. Listen up. She told you. She gave you permission man. What are you so afraid of?"

"Stop."

"Chase, you're my best friend man. It's time."

Chase sat still for a long time. Shifting his gaze from the pebbles at his feet, to the distance that stretched out before him, to the vastness of space above him.

"It's—"

"What?"

"It's too overwhelming. Years ago I thought everything was in place. Really solid. You know. Then the world splits apart, cracks appear and it's like I lost everything."

"I know."

"Never thought— I just never thought— Where do I even begin?"

"Dude, I think you already did."

Chase laughed and leaned his head against the truck's door with a thud.

"I guess I did." He took a moment. "What was Sophie about? After I left."

"She's cool. I guess. She saw something was up and wanted in. Who knows."

"She's not for me. She's fun, but she's not for me."

"Does she know that?"

"Sure she does. Made it pretty clear after the clambake."

"She's got a thing for you. Always has."

"It's the uniform man. It's just the uniform."

"I don't think so."

Both men where silent for a while and let the rhythm of the waves lull them into richer corners.

"She's something—" Chase began.

"She can be wild. That's for sure."

Chase looked at Connor. "I'm not talking about Sophie."

"Ohh— We're going there huh?" He picked up a twig at his feet and began peeling the bark, abstractedly waiting for Chase to spill.

"Lorelei. She's not my type at all, you know? But—"

"Uh huh." He picked a dry strip away from the twig and rolled it between his fingers.

"She's, um, weird. You know? But not weird. And not just the flower thing either. It's like, she's— I don't know. What is it about her?" He laughed a little as he tried to label his conflicting ideas. "She's really short. Shortest woman I know. But what is that? Nothing. It's nothing. She's small. But not small." He paused. "Jesus. What am I talking about? Small and not small? God." He paused and tried again. "She's not small at all. It's in her. Um. She's— well. She's not afraid of anything that's for sure. So she's—"

"Brave?"

"Well yes. She's all alone. Parents dead, no family. And she moves into this crazy old house and revives a bakery—on her own. But that's not it either. She's really funny too. Makes me laugh harder than I ever have in my life. And she's—"

"Yeah?" Connor waited.

Chase paused a moment. Both men knew how to fill in the unutterable words, so words were no longer necessary.

"So what do I do? Is this like dating? Like high school dating?" He stressed the word *dating* with a slight sarcastic edge. "Like going steady? Jesus. I'm too old for this."

"Chase. You're overthinking this. Yes it's a date. Ask her out again go have some fun."

"Like a drive-in? The soda shop?" His sarcasm was growing.

"Well, from the stories you've told me, sounds like a perfect first date would be breaking into the bank."

Chase laughed hard. "Ha! I know, right? Can you believe that?" He shook his head at the memory.

"Just make sure you clean up the flowers man. That would be a dead giveaway!"

"I know. What was that? What am I doing?"

"Chase. You don't have a choice. You're interested right?"

"Yeah"

"You like being with her, right?"

"Yeah."

"And she makes you laugh, right?"

"Hell yes!"

"Buddy, you're screwed."

"But—"

"There are no buts. Not anymore. Just a lot of excuses and delays. So she makes it rain flowers. Hell, my wife has a fortune-telling parlor in our house. Her Pop-pop paints nudes, and I watch everything and slurp it all up by the bucketful, man. By the bucketful. Stop waiting for your life to begin again. It already has! It began the moment you saw her Keds in the bakery window."

Chase laughed. "Aw hell. You're right. I'm screwed."

"Dude, you're smiling. What gives?"

"Get a rake. This town is going to drown in flowers." And Chase knew that when the flowers fell, he'd dive in headfirst.

Leaning his head against the truck, he smiled widely and decided Connor was right. His life had already begun and it was time to find a pair of white Keds.

Size twelve, men's.

Chapter 12

Sophie sat in her Buick and blew dull, grey smoke from her lungs. It tasted old this morning, like a lifetime turned to ash. Even crushing the cigarette in the car's ashtray became work. There were so many butts and the ash was so deep, she couldn't find a solid base and her cigarette just sank into the mess unsatisfactorily. No pleasing crunch of dry tobacco, no satisfying snap of ripped cigarette paper. A soft landing instead of the anticipated crush that gave her such pleasure.

She lit another cigarette and watched the bakery across the street. She slouched down a bit in her car seat, disgusted. It was early morning, but from the looks of it, Lorelei had been at work for hours. Every now and then, Sophie saw her blur through the store front, making coffee, refilling glass cookie jars, stocking shelves, then she'd disappear into the back for long stretches.

Customers arrived, some with kids. One had a dog he tied to the porch railing who took a few sloppy gulps from the water bowl Lorelei kept outside for thirsty pups. They all left the shop with the same brown bakery boxes tied up with red twine, a waxy bag or two. And here's the thing that aggravated Sophie the most—they all smiled and waved over their shoulders as they hopped down the porch steps. Content, fulfilled, with armfuls of delicacies. The bakery was a success and became the new hot-spot in Cobweb Corners.

She blew another jet of acrid smoke through the Buick's side window.

She gazed caustically over the house and bakery. Well, not a house at all. More like a rickety tenement made from toothpicks and witch's hair, straight out of a child's nightmare of nineteenth-century England. "Damn place outta be condemned," she mumbled.

She took a long pleasing drag from her cigarette and held it in her lungs. She loved watching the tip glow red. A pinprick of heat. It gave her a mooring, a temporary place to land despite the burn, and she had resided there for the past fifteen years.

She thought of Chase and the night she watched him cry in the parking lot. She had stayed in the shadows of Thoreau's Pub and watched from a distance. She saw his back and shoulders shaking in the parking lot and knew that protected stance all too well. He had kept it together for over a year, and if she waited long enough, she could be the one to heal that pain. She'd always been there for him. Even at Franny's funeral, her eyes never left his face. She followed every betraying wrinkle at the edges of his eyes, the lips he held too firmly, as though if he let go, he'd never recover.

His face haunted her for months after that. No one should go through that alone. She made it her mission to ignite his smile every moment she had. So what if it amounted to a wink, a free plate of Buffalo wings, a "law enforcement discount" she just made up. She knew he'd notice, and when he did, she'd be ready.

And now, this perky little baker.

She took another pull from her cigarette. The time had come. She grabbed her bulky purse and got out of the car. She wouldn't be mean. She wouldn't be angry. She'd just let this kid know that Chase had been hurt before.

Yeah, that's what she'd say.

He'd been hurt and he was not available. And it would be best for everyone if Lorelei would just back off.

She'd compliment her cute little store so she didn't come across too mean. But she'd be firm. Maybe even hold her eyes a long time, like she saw in her mother's favorite Joan Crawford movies. Not confrontational, but direct, knowing and powerful, the height of female sophistication (or so she believed).

She got out of her car, tossed the cigarette on the sidewalk, and stamped it out like it was an ant.

The house loomed over her and she tried her best to ignore her racing heart as she walked up the porch steps.

The place was looking cute. Too cute almost. She actually thought a glass of ice coffee on the porch might be nice some morning and a good book. A book? *Who am I kidding, I don't ever read books.*

The screen door opened with the peal of a small bell. Delicate and pleasing. *Sounds like that damn thing would summon Tinkerbell tossing pixie powder all over the freakin' place,* she thought with a bitter edge.

But it was the bakery aroma that stopped her in her tracks.

Warm cinnamon and vanilla curled through the air on wisps of rich coffee. Apple pie and honey rich crusts settled on her shoulders and caressed her dry lungs, bringing relief to a landscape that only inhaled regret and held lost opportunities like a miser.

But there was something else. Some unidentifiable scent from the childhood of happier kids. Orange maybe? Orange blossoms and cream? Soft, serene, and quietly, like an unseen guest who had always resided in her heart, Sophie realized she was missing something. Not an object like her glasses or a reliable car, but something deeper, more elemental. It shook her to the core and she suddenly felt cheap and insincere. She didn't realize she still held the screen door in her hand.

"Morning, Sophie. Happy to see you here!" Lorelei shouted from behind the counter. Bright and wide awake, she radiated light.

Holy hell, it's Little Mary Sunshine she gagged to herself. She suddenly wished for a dozen cigarettes, all tied together like a giant's fat cigar so she could drown in that nicotine haze and spread dry ash over the cutesy pixie-land floor beneath her feet, and then wash it down with a double gin martini.

"Morning, Lorelei," she said with a forced smile. "Just thought I'd stop in." She was trying her best to remain dignified, but she feared the rapid heartbeat under her blouse would give her away, like the body under the floorboards in that horrid Poe story she remembered from high school, beating so loudly it forced the murderer to confess his crime. Even back then, she thought that guy was a weak idiot.

"Can I get you a cup? The coffee's real good this morning. I made it a little stronger than usual, and you know what?" Lorelei whispered, like a secret shared between sisters. "This morning? I added just a dash of cinnamon to the coffee grounds. Do you believe it? I did. That's a big Southern secret, so don't tell nobody."

Oh! Really? Wouldn't you just. How amazingly cute. Why I won't tell a soul. Sophie ignored the desire to choke and said simply, "Umm, smells good."

She turned away from Lorelei and gazed at the delicacies in front of her as she tried to gather her thoughts. Bringing up the topic of backing off Chase in this place of sugars and sweets was like her parents bringing up their divorce at her seventh birthday party.

She paused.

Where did that come from? She hadn't thought about that in years and here it was, a visit from an unwelcome guest she tried to keep hidden deep in her pockets.

"Miss Sophie, are you okay?"

Sophie shook the ancient memory from her head and looked at the sincere face across the counter. "I'm fine. I'm fine kiddo. Just a late night. Listen, I want to talk about—"

"Let me get you a cup. Looks like you could use one. You want a warm cruller too? Just pulled them from the oven a few minutes ago."

And before Sophie could protest, she discovered a hot mug of coffee thrust in her hands, and a warm, crusty cruller was pushed across the counter on a vintage red plate.

She stared at the cruller, golden edges crisp as old onion skins, only sweeter. Honeycomb drizzled over flaky, paper thin pastry.

This kindness.

That kind of thing.

It was all a little overwhelming. Taking a sip of the rich coffee, she closed her eyes and tried to focus. Her intention was diminishing in the sugary daydreams in front of her.

Stay strong girl.

"Do you want to take something home?" Lorelei asked softly.

"No no. It looks all too sweet for me," she struggled to respond.

"Here, try a piece of this." Lorelei lifted the glass cloche from a dozen or so morsels of plain yellow cake. They were the only thing in the entire bakery that was not decorated.

Plain. Unadorned. Simple.

"Oh no. No. I couldn't."

"Go on, Sophie. Just try one. They're remarkable. It's a treat."

If I make it out of here without falling into a insulin coma I'll be amazed.

"Well, just one, if you insist." Sophie chose the smallest piece on the plate and popped the soft sponge into her mouth, where it slowly melted into song.

"Well? What do you think. Not too sweet is it?"

Sophie just stood there, silent and stoic. She swallowed the betraying smile that would give her away, for her taste buds were exploding in rapture. She let the songs of subtle vanilla drip down her throat and float through her lungs. She stood still for a few moments and lost herself in a wave of what became lavender light oozing into her core. It was remarkable.

"Well? How's that taste?"

She mumbled softly, "Little girl. It's like—" *I'm a little girl again*—and she had to tighten to resist the tears that she knew could soon follow.

She swallowed once.

Twice.

And then once more.

Under that hardened core, her insides sang, *More please! A thousand bites just like that one! Oh I could bathe in the breath of vanilla chai just like that! Drip it over my shoulders and kiss of cocoa hot cinnamon with rain and love and my child oh my child of orange spice and sweet tangles of hair and mama's kisses and—*

She opened her eyes, and the moment slipped away. She shoved it deep within her pockets where she kept memories too full, too sad, too long ago.

"Sophie?"

With a soft breath she said, "That was nice."

"Sometimes trying something plain helps people choose

what kind of pastry to buy. What did you taste?"

"Oh, just plain cake, very nice," she said.

Liar! It was like—

"Those look nice. What are they?" Sophie pointed to a shelf filled with luxurious cupcakes. Clouds of orange icing floated upon each delicate cake, and to keep them from leaving the earth altogether, a candied sprig of lime peel grounded them onto the fluted paper baking cup.

"I just made them. Something new! A little wild but totally yummy. They're Mango-Lime-Jalapeño cupcakes. The jala—"

"I'll take them."

"Wait what?"

"I'll take them."

"Sophie, there are over two dozen here. How many do you want?"

"All. I'll take them all." Sophie reached into her purse and pulled out a wad of cash. Her fight or flight instinct kicked in and flight was currently in overdrive.

"What do I owe you?"

"Well, I'll get them packed up for you real nice. They're two-fifty each, but I discount per dozen. I'll also add a few *profiteroles* on the house. You'll like them."

Sophie picked through the bills, and tossed away the odd gum wrapper and paperclip that inevitably found their way into her purse. She tossed the cash on the counter and left, her arms stacked with four bakery boxes she had never intended to buy and had even less intention to eat. And so, she fled.

Her car suddenly felt old, tired, and giving in to the hardscrabble years that had journeyed through its frame. She sat in the front seat. Feeling a bit too dazed for a cigarette, she stared at the bakery boxes beside her.

What the hell was that?

She swiped the tears away from her face and putting the car in drive, she slowly drove away.

She decided to skip buying the usual flowers for the receptionist at Fordhook's Home.

She had over two dozen cupcakes that were more beautiful than any bouquet she could ever buy.

A small smile crept across her face as she imagined walking

into the reception room to deliver the beautiful gifts that sat next to her. She rolled down the window and turned on the radio. Joni Mitchell's voice carried her along as a cool relief flooded her core.

Her smile was particularly wide that morning.

Chapter 13

"Mornin' Sophie. What brings you out here on a weekday?" Olivia sat behind the receptionist counter, and glanced up briefly when she heard the hush of the glass door slide open.

"Morning, Liv. I was in the neighborhood and wanted to stop by. How is she today?" She shifted the bakery boxes in her arms, looking for a clear spot on the counter for them.

"Same as ever, same as ever. Sweet as can be and never brings us any trouble at all. She is a sweet thing." Olivia smiled kindly. "Whatcha got?" Her eyes widened at the sight of the bakery boxes.

"Well, instead of flowers this month, I decided to get you all a little treat. Hand them out as you see fit."

"Morning, Sophie." Tucker stopped by in his orderly, baby blue scrubs, pushing a large cart covered with residents' lunches. "Never seen you out here on a weekday. What's up?"

"Hey, Tucker. Just came by for a visit. That's all." She tried hard not to notice the way his short sleeved scrub hugged his solid biceps. Tucker was a hottie, that's for sure. And that full lipped smile? *I could drown in a smile like that,* she thought.

"Look, I brought you all a surprise," she said and gently untied a bakery box, the red twine slipping through her fingers like fine silk. "We have this new baker in town. And when I saw these cupcakes, I couldn't resist. Just look!"

She ceremoniously lifted the lid and the scent of spun sugar and tropical cocktails rose from the magical space.

"Holy moly!" Tucker hummed deeply. "Those things smell incredible. What kind are they?"

"Who knows," Sophie replied. "Something orangey. They

looked so pretty I couldn't resist. Take one!"

"Naw, don't waste one on me. Give mine to Olivia."

"Tucker, I bought almost thirty of them! And she tossed in a few other custardy things for free, take one!"

Sophie reached into the box delicately. "Here, Liv, you get the first one. Enjoy it with your coffee."

Olivia's eyes glimmered as she received the light cupcake. Moist and firm, the cupcake sat regally on her desk, a queen among papers and pens.

"Tucker, take this one, go on! Tuck it away on your cart and have it with lunch." Sophie smiled as she flirtatiously handed him the exotic cake, and resisted making a joke about hot buns and icing on the cake. "Now, let me take one, and you guys can hand out the rest to anyone who could use one, okay? Just put them in the luncheon room or something. Don't go to any extra trouble. Tucker? Hand me a plate and a fork, would you?"

With the class of a five-star waiter, the buffed guy presented her with a bright white plate. With a flair, he wiped it with a napkin to make it sparkle, and handed her a plastic fork as though he were presenting her with the glass slipper he always knew would fit.

"You're such a goof," she said. "But I love it, I really do."

Placing the cupcake upon the plate made the room glow slightly with an iridescent splendor. It felt good. Orange tones and creamy richness had a way of restoring everyone to childhood summers, and today was no different. It infected them all.

It felt good to bring simple smiles to people.

She walked down the hall and called over her shoulder, "Those things are loaded with sugar. Watch the diet restrictions."

And turning the corner, she was out of sight.

Sophie entered the quiet room, shut the door softly behind her, and looked at the silhouette in the wheelchair. The old woman faced the window. Still, frozen in time, and silent. It was always the same. For the last five years, no change, no communication, no thoughts registered on the old woman's blank face.

Sophie placed the treat on the metal dining tray and rolled it in front of the old woman. She sat with a defeated sigh, and began the routine she had performed nearly every week for the past five years.

"Hi, Mama," she said in her best, well-rehearsed happy voice. "I brought you a treat today." Removing the crimped baking paper from the edges was a feat of resistance and personal control. The cake was so moist it stuck to her fingertips and begged to be licked from edges and creases. The frosting tipped a fingernail or two, highlighting the garish color she chose last week. Purple passion. It was all wrong when set against such remarkably natural colors that Lorelei created.

"We have a new baker in town, Mama. Remember old Adelaide's bakery, way out by the lighthouse?" She continued to talk, peeling away the baking paper like a fine skin from an exotic fruit. "Well, her niece moved in, and reopened the shop. Young lady from the south somewhere. It looks real nice too. She hasn't changed a thing. You'd love it, Mama. Here, try a bite of this. So pretty, isn't it? Looks like a pretty cloud."

The old woman sat still and watched with sleepy eyes as Sophie raised a small forkful of orange sponge and delicate icing to her mouth.

"Here you go. Try a bite of this. Looks delicious."

There was no reaction. There never was.

Sophie gently placed the fork against her mother's lips.

"Try it, Mama. You always loved cake."

The old woman gently kissed the frosting with subtle attempts at tasting it. Over the years, feeding her was becoming a longer process and required more and more time. Didn't matter to Sophie. The hours with her mom filled her with gratitude. The sorrow followed later. Usually on the drive home. But for now? Today? This moment? She'd treat her mom to a lovely small cake that looked like it was made for a fairy princess.

The woman licked her lips and leaned forward, taking the delicate forkful and closed her dry lips around it.

"Wow. Mama. That was a big bite. Want another?" She held

another forkful of the orange sponge for her mother. She leaned forward and accepted the cake into her mouth. As she held the sponge against her tongue, she leaned back in her chair and closed her eyes, like she was tasting a distant memory.

Sophie watched, intently. Something was going on. She watched as her mother swallowed the cake, licked her lips, and though her mother's eyes were closed, Sophie saw there was activity going on inside that recessed mind. Small wheels were turning and thin connections were being made. It was a subtle dance, and though it was small, grace was evident.

She leaned forward for another bite, which Sophie supplied. Orange frosting stained the woman's lips and Sophie watched as she let the cake dissolve on her tongue.

"Butterflies—" The voice was soft and distant, like a fragment of a forgotten song heard through a faraway veil.

"Mama?"

"Baby—your butterflies."

"Mama? What—?" Sophie froze in her chair.

The woman with icing lipstick opened her eyes gently and the two, mother and daughter, stared at each other as though the irreparable gulf that had separated them for years had receded into a small verdant pasture.

Her voice was dry and soft. "Baby girl, you always loved butterflies. What happened to them? Where did you put them?"

"Mama—is that you? Mama?" Sophie ignored the tears streaming down her face and grasped her mother's hand. Boney and thin, she held it gently like she were comforting a wounded bird.

"Mama, how—?"

"Baby girl. Why are you so sad?"

"Mama, you're speaking! My mama—" The tears were choking her.

"You're a good girl. Be kind, baby. You need to get your butterflies back. Okay?" Her voice was dry and weak.

Sophie held her mother's hand tightly, and the years slipped away as though she were a little girl again.

"Baby, you have to forgive," she said. "Find your butterflies baby. Promise."

Sophie could barely speak. "Promise! I promise. Mama—"

Her mother reached out and caressed her face. Gazing intently into her daughter's eyes she said, "My baby girl. What a pretty woman you've become."

Sophie held her mother's hand to her lips and kissed it greedily, never tiring of her task.

"Mama, my mama, are you back? Is this real? I need to get the nurse—"

"Those butterflies—" Her voice was diminishing.

Panicked, Sophie shouted. "Wait! Mama, wait. I need to get the nurse!" Cupcake and plate in hand, she ran to the door and yelled in to the hall, "Nurse! Olivia! Come quick! Tucker! Somebody! It's amazing! She's talking!"

Within moments, Olivia and a resident nurse stood in the doorway, breathless and wide-eyed.

The nurse hurried toward the old woman who looked up with fading, recessed eyes.

"Mrs. Anderson? How are we doing today?" She asked calmly and began the routine of checking the old woman's pulse.

"'Liv, it was incredible!" Sophie stammered, "She started talking to me like she was fine. Like it was yesterday. She recognized me! She knew who I was! Mama? How are you doing?"

"She seems fine," the nurse said. "Pulse is a little fast, but nothing to be concerned about. Mrs. Anderson, how are you doing today?"

There was no answer.

"Look who came to visit today! And she brought you a cupcake. Isn't that sweet?"

The nurse turned the wheelchair around to face the two women in the doorway. Though no evidence was present, Sophie could see her mother's light recede.

"We'll take her down the hall for some checkups," the nurse told her. "Sometimes moments like this creep in. Her pulse is elevated so—Sophie? Sophie, did you hear me?"

Sophie didn't hear a word. In fact, she could barely breath. She stared at her mother's window in wide-eyed wonder.

The sunlight became alive and danced across the

shimmering glass surface.

Dozens of magnificent butterflies gathered and rhythmically beat their gossamer wings against the window. Brilliant yellow wings, tipped with fiery orange and velvet black. Reflected in the glass, their number doubled and the gently beating wings fanned the newly departing spirit and gave joy to her elemental release.

Sophie dropped the plate and it shattered against the floor into a million fragments of cream colored tears, highlighted by a brilliant cupcake sunset in the center.

Part 3: Early Autumn
Bake with Care

Chapter 14

Autumn in Cobweb Corners brings a taste of the chilly days ahead. Ocean waters turn crisper, nights become cooler, and campfires spot the beach with sparks of other people's lives and other people's journeys.

Lorelei sat comfortably in the sand. Her knees hugged to her chest, cotton dress wrapped tightly around them like a blanket. Bear at her side, she stared at the man across from her. The fire lit his rugged face in amber and orange tones where it glowed like a protective lion, though, up close, his eyes softened, transformed by the magical woman in his gaze. She knew he was trying to tell her something important, but he was stumbling on the words. She smiled as she recognized his awkwardness and she wondered about this man whom she had grown to love.

The hurt in his life was still evident in the edges of his eyes, but there was a new life there too. She saw it when he smiled. She heard it when he laughed. And she loved it when he showed her his new white sneakers, size twelve.

"The nights get so cold up here. Easy to tell fall is on its way," she said, trying to break the silence. "Back home? In Kentucky? Nothing like this. Just rainy and grey." She gazed into the fire for a moment. "Don't know why I said 'home.'"

She furrowed her brow a bit. "That place was never home. Just a sloppy trailer in the woods. Never felt like I belonged there. Never felt like I belonged anywhere really." She looked up at Chase. "I feel that now. Here. That crazy bakery and that lighthouse." She took a risk. "You especially."

The two looked at each other. Curious. Their stories and

histories were written in creases and subtle scars they carried. They smiled, for in the rhythmic waves on the shore, they heard the possibility of washing away those ancient fears in their newfound journey—together.

He gazed silently. She watched the subtle movement of his brow, the minute flicker of his eyes, the edges of his mouth rise in a tender smile. It filled her heart.

"Chase, why are you so distant tonight? Are you thinking about Fran?"

"No, no," he said from the edge of the world. "I'm not. I'm thinking about jumping."

"What?"

He took slight breath and shifted his weight. "I have these dreams," he told her. "I feel like I'm on the edge of the world and I want to jump off into—"

"Into?" she encouraged.

She watched him wrestle with words that seemed beyond his recognition.

"I don't know. I'm on the edge and it's terrifying. But below me, it isn't dark or anything like that. It actually seems safe. Like a soft landing I guess."

She sat still and listened. She knew he had traveled a long way to get to these words. So, in her gaze, patience walked hand in hand with love, and slowly, without judgement or need, she opened the space where words finally became possible.

With an unsure tremor in his voice, he continued. "The thing is, I'm not sure how to begin—"

"Chase. Begin what? What is it?" She traced a few random designs in the sand. Maybe breaking eye contact would make it easier for him. Besides, she loved the way the cool, damp sand felt against her fingers. Like soft brown sugar.

"Lorlei, look at me."

She did. Her eyes lit warmly by the crackling fire light and magnified the magical soul within her.

"Baby," he said, "I know what it is now. In those dreams, I want to fall, but I'm terrified. I'm on the edge."

"What are you afraid of? Falling into what?"

"Lorelei. It's you," he told her as a wide smile of recognition grew across his warm lips. "I don't know where you came from. But I'm hooked." He laughed a small awkward snort and looked down at his feet, barely able to continue. "You came out of nowhere. I never expected it—you—this. This thing we have. I didn't think is was possible. Ever." He paused.

She could see he was choking on the words a little.

"I was lucky when I found Franny. I know that. And you need to know that I loved her, deeply."

Lorelei nodded. She understood and was not jealous. She felt honored to hear about his ability to love.

"But to find this twice? You?" He thought for a moment. "You amaze me." He laughed aloud for the words felt real and true. He held her eyes like a man who finally reached a long desired shoreline. "You really do. Just say when, and I'll leap off that cliff. I'll soar off that thing!"

"Chase—"

"You flew into my life when I never expected I could smile again. Ever. Your white sneakers waving in that damn window, it was like a surrender flag. Really. I think you may have saved me. My life." The words, finally identified, flooded his core and relief washed over his senses like a long-awaited shower in a parched desert. "I really do."

Lorelei laughed. Embarrassed, but also proud. She was melting into this man's words and the richness of his voice flowed through her core, filling her with a presence she had never felt before. She had finally arrived, and waves of relief overpowered her.

"Chase—"

"I'm not done. Baby, I surrender. I don't know what you have, but whatever magic it is, I surrender." He inched toward her on his knees. "I want more and more of it. Cover me with your flowers! Let me feast on them. Would you? Can I? Please?"

In the warmth of the firelight, she saw glistening tracks running down his cheeks. Disrupted by his wide smile, the tears were joyful trails springing from a journey too painful to recount, too deep to ignore.

"Oh my God, Chase. You're so beautiful," she said in wonder. She had never seen a man cry before, and never thought a man could be beautiful. The sight filled her with love. For this man, on his knees, crying in the fire light, made her recognize that the world was good. That love was good, and all that lay behind her, her days of isolation and loneliness were through.

"Now, I have to know. Are you into this?"

"What?" She could barely breathe.

"Are you into this?" he repeated softly. He sounded as though he was asking for her permission to fall in love with her.

And he was.

"Chase," she said holding his tear stained face in her small hands, "I'm into this. One-hundred percent, three bags full! Yes, oh yes, I'm into this."

And without warning, she threw herself to her feet and stretched her arms up over her head and shouted into the late August sky, "I'm into this!" Her voice rose into the night like fireflies. Sparkling and dividing into brilliant, soft pinpricks of light, sound waves became diamonds glittering in moonlight.

With perfect balance, she removed a shoe and tossed it over her shoulder in the sand. Laughing like a child on Christmas morning, she tossed the other shoe behind her.

And with a laughter that rang over Cobweb Corners, she ran to the shoreline and in the cold shallow surf, began a dance of absolute celebration. She pounded her toes into the cold waves that washed away a filthy trailer in Kentucky. She twirled in joyous circles as her cotton dress fanned into a blur of milky blue. Arms wide enough to hold the entire galaxy, she spun around again and again. Whooping and hollering into the deep night, she released her isolation and let it wash away in the waves that hit her thighs with silvery delight.

"Chase!" she called from her wet, wet, world, "Do you love me?"

He stood and shouted, "Love you? Baby I'm crazy about you!"

She squealed into the night air. "You hear that, stars?" She splashed through the waves, soaking her dress, water glistening upon her face. "He loves me! I am someone to be loved!" And she spun in magical circles not caring who saw her joyous release.

Bear barked from the shoreline. "Bear! You hear that? I'm loved!" She kicked water in a thousand directions, more beautiful than the Trevi fountain, more joyous than the Rainbow Falls.

She stopped, breathless and stared at the man on the beach. "And I love, too!" she yelled into the firmament above. "I love you, Chase. I do."

Water dripped from her long hair, from her chin and her nose. She was breathing heavily as though she had run a great distance, and indeed, she had. Cold sea water swept down her neck, caressed her chest and dripped from the hem of her dress as she stood in the twilight waves. The transport had passed, and left a whole, awakened woman in its place.

"Chase," she said over the gentle waves, "I'll take whatever you have to give and I'll return it in abundance. In abundance! Oh my lord you are so beautiful."

She began the slow walk toward the dry man on land, and she knew when she reached him, they would make love on the shore, and she would never return to the old life she had known before.

When the lovemaking came, she wasn't prepared. Nothing had prepared her for this. She knew sex was supposed to be wonderful, but she didn't know it could be healing, life affirming, and she gave herself freely. She never knew it could bridge the gap between what separates and divides. She never knew it could make the lost become whole again. She learned this in his arms, in the sand, under an autumn moon and as they became lost in each other, a small fire dwindled beside them. It spit and sputtered, and though low, its warmth carried them away in amber arms.

And when they both cried out, Bear lifted his head from the shoreline where he sat, gave a small, satisfying howl and, mesmerized by the rhythmic waves, he sighed himself to sleep.

Chapter 15

The house sat in the distance, watching the new lovers on the beach, all the while holding a new secret in her own heart.

A dangerous secret.

Even Bluebeard got it wrong. That much we know.

Temptation is a murderous device. It leads the wonderer into dangerous quests, and once satiated, the desire starts all over again. Stronger. Starving to be fulfilled. Ravenous even.

And Bluebeard's twisted desire killed him. That much we know.

Twirling a key nervously in his boney fingers, the young man in a dirty cap sat in the darkened bakery and waited.

As she approached her house, she didn't need to leave a bread crumb trail for she knew the path to her gingerbread home. Holding the strong man's hand in her own, she also knew they would share her bed tonight. But this time, there would be no fumbling in the sheets, no awkward touches or tentative caresses. Their desire fulfilled, her bed would contain the warm embrace of satiated lovers, wrapped in warmth, contentment, and the security of knowingness.

Even Little Red Riding Hood stood nude before the wolf. And Red knew to truly be awakened, one must be consumed. Totally. When she faced the wolf, the journey stared back with hungry eyes and a salivating grin.

When dreams collapse, what is left?

The awful awakening. The reckoning, the reunion with the

uninvited guest.

Lorelei swung open the kitchen door. "Chase, have a seat. I'm starved and soaked. Let me get some dry clothes and goodies from the shop. Any requests?"

"Guess you don't have a cheerleader's outfit," he said with a grin.

"I'm talking food, not clothes! My lord! And no. The secondhand shop was all out. Maybe I'll ask Sophie. We're about the same size," she said with a wry smile as she ran upstairs.

Not caring about appearance, she tossed on a pair of worn jeans, an oversized tee, and she hurried to the dark bakery. She hollered over her shoulder, "Chase? You want a few of those chewy oatmeal pecan bars you like so much? Milk's in the fridge."

Flicking on the lights, she reached for a the cookie jar— and screamed.

"Forget something, Lorelei?" The young man said with a hint of acid in his voice. He sat at the small cafe table, bakery keys dangling from a finger. "Looks like you forgot your keys." The smile was sickening. Dirty teeth, slouched shoulders, stained shirt.

"Lorelei? You okay?" Chase shouted.

She stared at Beeker, heart beating loudly. "Fine! I'm fine. Just a mouse. That's all. Just a mouse lookin' for another handout." She looked her brother in the eye and said lowly, "Get out. This is mine. You have no place here."

He laughed. "You seem to be forgettin' something, baby girl. You have a ton of my money." He leaned back in the cafe chair, balancing it perfectly upon two legs and enjoyed the show written in his sister's eyes. "You stole m'dog too! Now, how about that?"

"Beeker! I never spent a dime of—"

"Lorelei? What's this?" Chase stood in the doorway, hand instinctively on his hip where his holster would have been.

She looked at Chase, eyes wide with concern. She saw Beeker, cocky, arms folded behind his head as he rocked in the chair. Smiling as though he had won the grand prize.

She knew she lost. The Big Bad Wolf followed her to her

door and sat before her, salivating with victory.

She was Bluebeard's wife, bloody key in her hand.

Even Goldilocks was a thief.

"Lorelei, are things okay? Who is this?"

The breath she took was the last of her life, for she knew when the words came, she would lose everything.

"Chase," she said bravely, "this is my brother, Beeker."

"That's twin brother," he added in mock pride. "Who the hell are you and what are you doing in my aunt's house?"

"This is my house, Beeker! So stop! Just stop all this!" she yelled desperately.

"Stop what? I'm stopping nuthin' till I git my money and m'dog back! Where is he anyway? Bear?" he yelled into the darkened doorway.

"Lorelei what is this? What's going on? You never said you had a brother—" Chase stood stoically, confusion spreading across his face.

Beeker laughed. "Hoowee! He don't know? This your new boyfriend, Lala? Mister, seems like my sister has been keeping secrets again. Right, Lala? He know about the money you stole?"

She stood firmly. The ravens finally came home to roost and found the rookery was rotten to the core.

"Beeker," she said calmly, "Chase. Wait here a moment would you both?" And within seconds, she was flying up the old staircase, banister whizzing by her like a film strip in fast forward. In moments she was on her knees digging under her bed. Arms flying blindly through the dusty space until they found their intended target. An old backpack filled with rolls of cash.

"There you are," she hissed through gritted teeth. "Time to meet your maker."

She flew herself down the staircase, hitting every other step in bare feet, grabbed the door frame and tossed herself around the corner and found herself breathless in the bakery, stuck between two chapters. Beeker, and her past of want and neglect, and Chase, the future of dreams fulfilled.

She stared at the two men who looked at her in wonder and fear.

She began.

"Chase. I'm sorry baby. I am. I came here hoping for a new life in this shop. I'm so sorry. I thought I could leave everything behind me. Everything I hated." And she looked at Beeker. "Even you, Beeker. I took care of you, fed you, even bailed you out and what did I get in return? Huh? Nothing!"

She held the backpack tightly, her fingers curling like iron spiders. "All I ever got from you is worry, hateful remarks. Ugly guys showing up at all hours shouting, 'Beeker! I need some powder!" She reached into the pack and grabbed a roll of cash in her fist. "Beeker! I need some blow!" She hurled the roll at her brother and hit him square in the jaw, like a rock. "Beeker! I need some weed!" She threw another roll, which cracked against his forehead. "Beeker! I need some Jack!" Another roll flew across the room and hit his chest. "Beeker, I need!" A roll slammed against the window. A roll hit the door and exploded in a shower of rolled bills.

Dumping the remaining rolls on the floor, she kicked them as though they were snakes and knew their venomous bite was deadly. "I'm done! Right now! I. Am. Done!" She pounded on her chest.

She walked over to her brother, surprised by the hurt in his face—and she slapped him.

Hard.

"That hurt? That's nothing compared to life in a filthy trailer with you."

She turned to apologize to Chase, and she found an empty space where he once stood.

He was gone.

She knew it was over.

Exhausted, she looked at her brother who suddenly appeared a mouse at the foot of a giant. "That's it. That's all I got Beeker, and once again, you took the best of me."

She looked out of the bakery door. "You have the keys. It's yours," she said with simple finality. "I've got nothing left Beeker. You've got it all. You won." With a small breath, she laughed. "Funny. I thought I could bury you. But here you are standing before me, like daddy's shotgun, ready to fire at anything. Trouble is, you got no aim and you destroy anything close to you."

The darkness on the bakery porch was consuming. "So. That's it Beeker. You found me. You caught me. Took you a while. But I gotta say, your aim is much sharper than daddy's. More deadly too."

"Lorelei, let me—"

"Stop! There is not a single word I ever want to hear from you. Okay? And some how I know I'll read an obituary about you. Maybe next week, maybe next year, maybe ten years. Overdose, shot, dead somehow. Hard thing is, wish I could say I don't care. But I do. And that's what really hurts, Beeker. I know you'll never understand it." She paused. "Bakery opens at six AM." She held in her tears, firm as iron. "Folks around here like a dash of Cinnamon in the coffee."

"Lala—"

"Don't! No. Not now. Not ever." She began to walk out the door. "I never spent a dime of your poisoned money. It is poison you know, and it's killing us both." And she gently opened the old screen door and stepped onto the porch. She expected the floor to be more unsure, softer somehow, like she was walking across a new landscape. But it held her firmly and guided her down the weathered porch steps where she found the ground was solid beneath her feet.

Charged. Resentful in fact.

Without a thought of her journey, she found herself once again in the driver's seat of her VW. She slowly drove away.

Refusing to watch the gingerbread bakery recede in her rear view mirror, she began to cry.

Chapter 16

Heading south out of Cobweb Corners, Route 12 meanders through massive pine and hemlock forests, healthy and robust, providing the traveler with deep, green scented shade. Crystal streams weave beside tall trunks whose roots are fed with spring water so clear, the locals swear by their restorative powers.

But on nights like this, the dark overwhelms the traveler. The canopy of limbs overhead blots out the moonlight and soaks the air like black ink upon wool. Thick, heavy, drowning. That kind of night.

A VW Bug chugged through the darkness along this route, following the dim, sepia light it projected onto the dark road ahead. Its motor hummed along, confident, and followed each dip and turn of the isolated road. For the hundredth time, Lala swiped her wet sleeve across her face, attempting to dry her tear stained eyes and runny nose. Already soaked, her sleeve stubbornly refused to accept any more salty water from her face.

Searching for a dry tissue, she reached across to the glove compartment. One hand on the wheel, the other tugging the old latch that either stuck too much, or suddenly popped open from a minor pot hole bounce.

"C'mon you! Open," she muttered through a clenched jaw and fumbled with the lock.

It held tightly, stubborn and selfish.

She gave it a few hard whacks with her fist when she saw the whizz of the deer as it flew across her path.

She slammed the brakes and the tires squealed as the car

slid across the dark road. Lala screamed and the Bug spun off the side where it came to rest in a shallow ditch. The driver sat, breathing heavily in the stillness, and at last the bumpy journey came to a stop.

Nothing spectacular. A minor event really.

The deer paused for a gulp from the spring by the road, unaware of her brush with death. Lala watched the majestic animal. The animal drank, lifted her head, bent low and gulped again.

Lala leaned back against the headrest, whose dry fibrous stuffing crunched like ancient hay. *What am I going to do? Wish I could just follow that deer and dump everything in the river. Just let it all go.*

Putting the car in reverse, she guided the Bug out of the ditch. Old tires spun in the wet ground and the Bug rocked a bit.

"Oh shit."

She tried again and the wheels spun, kicking dirt and pebbles in a shower across the road.

"No!" she yelled. "C'mon you!"

Furious, she got out of the car to look at the problem. She knew how to get a car out of the mud. Easy. Life in the Kentucky hills taught her that. Plenty of pine boughs around for traction under the wheels. No problem.

Then she saw the tree trunk. Wedged under the bug, it suspended the front end a foot off the ground.

There was no way she could do this on her own.

She broke. Bent in half, she clutched the fender of the car, and slowly began sobbing into the night.

Beeker, shame, guilt, it all spilled out onto the isolated road.

A heaving breath wracked her body and bent double again. Chase, his arms, finally feeling safe at last. A home. A place to land.

All gone now.

She poured a shower of tears into the ditch that night. Body heaving in pain, twisted from her own lies and shamed at revealing the truth, the tears flowed freely and soaked the ground beneath her feet. She could cry all night and never release enough.

"Lorelei?"

"Huh?" She lifted her head and spun around.

"Girl, what is going on! Are you okay?" Sophie stood a few feet away, cigarette in her fingertips, her car idling in the distance.

"No, I'm not okay! Look at me. I'm a slobbery mess. My shirt is soaked with snot. My friggin' car is hung up in a ditch, and I didn't even kill that deer. No. I am not okay."

Sophie smiled.

Lorelei took a breath. "I didn't even hear you pull up." She attempted a failed swipe across her face, smearing tears over her swollen cheeks and getting her limp hair even wetter. "How'd you find me?"

"On my way home, saw your car in the ditch and a mess of a girl crying on the road side. Figure you needed a hand." She took a long pull from her cigarette whose tip glowed brilliantly in the dark. "What's going on?" She took another pull.

Lorelei watched as Sophie held the smoke in her lungs, like a powerful genie. The exhale was a lesson in strength. She blew the smoke from the corner of her lips with a perfectly aimed trajectory up where it dissipated into the night air above them both. Sophie's eyes shined like a siren.

"Give me one of them," Lorelei demanded.

"Kiddo, you don't smoke," Sophie laughed gently.

"I do now!" She reached out for one. She placed the tight cigarette in her thin lips and Sophie, smiling ruefully, sparked her lighter.

In a moment, the night became alive with a hot glow that illuminated their small circle in the New Hampshire woods, uniting them in the most ancient of rituals. Lorelei inhaled the searing smoke deep into her lungs where she held it like a dying breath.

And instantly doubled over and vomited in the ditch.

"Oh God, oh God," she mumbled as the tears started again. "I can't even do a cigarette right!"

"Girl. You just can't dive in and expect to become a smoker," Sophie chided. "Takes practice and determination to ruin a life" she added ruefully.

"Well, I got that down pat," Lorelei said on her knees,

wiping her fist across her mouth.

"I have water in the car. Let me get it for you. Because right now?" she added, "You look like Doris Day crash landed on the Island of Misfit Toys."

"Thanks, hit me when I'm down why don't you."

"Lorelei, look. Here's how it is," Sophie shouted from her car, "some of us were born to smoke. Some of us were born to bake. And you my friend are not a smoker. Take this." She approached Lorelei and held out a water bottle.

Lorelei stood tentatively and brushed the pebbles from her knees. "Thanks," she said as she twisted the cap open and took a few greedy gulps. Washing the bile and acrid smoke from her mouth, she took the first cleansing breath of the night.

"Your car is pretty stuck."

"Don't I know it—"

"How'd you get out here? You're a mess."

Lorelei couldn't believe her ears. "Yes, I'm a mess!" She shouted. "Of course I'm a mess!" She shouted more rapidly than a machine gun. "My freaking drug-dealer brother found me and Chase heard and thinks I stole the money! Which I didn't! But really I guess I did. Well, I took it—yes! But so what? I never spent it! And then Chase took off! So now he thinks that in addition to breaking and entering, I'm also a thief and then Beeker—"

"Hold it, hold it, slow down," Sophie cautioned. The story was getting too good and she didn't want to miss a beat. "One thing at a time. What brother? I swear you told me you didn't have any family," she said with an arched brow. "And money? Drug money? This is getting good." Sophie tapped the ash from her cigarette onto the street. "Where are you headed?"

"Nowhere. Got no place to go."

"How do you plan to get your car out of the ditch?"

Defeated, Lorelei shrugged.

Sophie took another long, languorous pull from her cigarette and looked at Lorelei. She flicked the butt expertly onto the gravel, stomped it out with a determine toe, and said. "Listen. Here's the plan. I'll call a guy I know with a tow truck. You're staying with me tonight, we'll get you back on the road tomorrow. Deal?"

"But—"

"No. That's the plan. Take it or sleep here tonight. What will it be?"

Lorelei looked at the confident woman in front of her. Sophie was direct, but help was offered and she decide to take it.

"Deal," she said.

"Good." Sophie whipped her cell phone from her purse like a covert spy on a mission and dialed.

"Hey Tucker? It's Sophie. How's your tow truck looking tonight?"

Lorelie saw her smile slightly as she listened to the disembodied voice. The smile grew across her lips. Calm and sweet, Lorelei knew that smile.

"Great," Sophie said. "Tucker, you're a doll. We're out on Route 12, just past the town spring. You'll see us. I've got enough cigarettes to send up a flare the size of a spaceship."

She held out the pack and winked at Lorelei.

Chapter 17

Lorelei woke with dry, foul mouth. She peeled open one sleepy, sandy eye and peeked at her surroundings. A sofa bed under her, a heavy afghan covering her, and large black lab on top.

"Waffles, get down!"

The dog jerked his head toward the kitchen, shaking the uncertain bed with its massive weight.

"Waffles! Leave that poor girl alone. Come eat your breakfast. Get down," the harsh voice demanded.

Pots crashed and banged, and Lorelei noticed the scent of strong coffee filling the space. And something else, too. Something sour and old. Dry acrid smoke haunted the blankets and pillows.

"Waffles!"

Brushing her hair from her sleepy face, Lorelei sat up in bed. It was all coming back. Sophie's living room, the ditch, getting sick in the road.

Beeker.

Chase.

"Oh no …" she whispered, and flung herself back onto the flat pillow.

"Well good morning sunshine! Looks like you could use a cuppa." Sophie leaned against the kitchen doorway wrapped in an oversized pink robe, coffee cup tight in her hands. "How about it kiddo. Coffee and some eggs?"

"Coffee sounds good," came the disembodied voice. "Thanks—"

"Coming right up." She disappeared into the kitchen and yelled over her shoulder. "There's a robe for you at the foot of the bed. You might have to brush off the dog hair. Haven't used it for a while. The dog likes to sleep on it." She hacked a solid cough. "Pretty day in store out there," she hollered, and followed with a mumble under her breath, "if you're into that sort of thing."

"What did I do yesterday? I feel hungover— Did I drink?"

"No girl," Sophie shouted from the kitchen, "something much worse—you stained your soul with one, pure and unaltered mentholated cigarette." She laughed and cracked some eggs, beating them with a fork. "Oh it was a black night it was. Black as a rook on a midnight flight across the sky— No turning back now." She laughed. "You're doomed."

Sophie stood in the doorway, beating the eggs and looking at Lorelei for a reaction, cigarette dangling from her dry lips. Seeing none, she said, "Lorelei, we gotta have a talk. Time to spill girl."

"Huh?"

Sophie headed back to the kitchen and Lorelei heard the sizzle of sloppy eggs hitting a greased pan. "You left more than some puke on the road last night," she hollered from the kitchen, "shouting all sorts of things about Chase, money, stolen money?" Sophie peeked around the corner. "You hear me? And a brother? I swear you told us you don't have any family. Am I right? Or am I making something up?"

Lorelei stayed silent.

"Seems to me there's a lot more to the mild-mannered baker than meets the eye."

"Will you stop saying that?"

"What?"

"All this Doris Day mild mannered miss prissy stuff. You said it last night and you're at it again. If you don't like me why did you bother to help me in the first place?"

"Easy kiddo! I'm just getting started," she hacked another deep cough. "No one with a heart would have seen your pathetic sight on the road last night and drove on by."

"Oh, so now you're claiming you have a heart?" She called back sarcastically.

Sophie stood in the doorway, breakfast plates in hand, and her face grew warm with appreciation. The two women stared at each other for a moment, and recognizing a similar fury in the other, liked what they saw, and called a truce.

"Here, breakfast is ready. Toss on the robe and come talk with me."

"No wisecracks?"

"None, Girl Scout's honor."

"That's a laugh. Since when were you—"

Sophie shot her a look.

"Sorry. You're right. Sorry." Lorelei swung her feet out of bed, tossed on the robe, and sat at the small breakfast table.

"I don't know why you're doing this. I'm a mess and—"

"Stop. Eat some food. And spill."

Lorelei picked up her fork and dove into the plate of scrambled eggs.

"There's some Sriracha for the eggs if you like them spicy," Sophie mentioned as she poured dark coffee in Lorelei's mug. The mug looked out of place on the table. A sunshiny pattern of rainbows and flowers grew around an obscenely happy cartooned cheerleader who shouted in pink bubblegum text, "I'm a morning girl!"

Lorelei looked at the mug and shot Sophie a dead pan glance. "Sorry," Sophie said. "I couldn't resist. It's so you." Held to her lips, her coffee cup could barely conceal her grin.

Lorelei shook a few blood red dots of hot sauce on the side of her plate and dove in. Toast buttered, coffee rich and dark, a few slabs of thick bacon, glistening with grease. "This is remarkable, thanks."

"I'm waiting."

"What for?"

"Spill!"

"I don't know where to start," she said as she played with her eggs distractedly. "It's too much and it's all swirling around."

"Oh, I don't know," Sophie said with ease. "How about the stolen money? Lorelei! What? You stole money?"

"Oh gosh. I said that? Really?"

"Spill!" Sophie's elbows where pressed firmly on the table. Her extra large coffee cup gripped tightly in her hands and a greedy smile on her face that said she could listen all day if necessary.

"Okay. So. My brother found me."

"What do you mean 'found'? You ran away? With stolen money?"

"Yes. Well, no. It's bad, okay? I left the key under my mattress and that's why Chase thinks I broke into the bakery, which I didn't. But yes, so okay. I broke into the lighthouse, and boy was that awkward. Then—"

"Wait a minute," Sophie gently took Lorelei's coffee from her. "No more caffeine for you. You're flying. Now, slow down. You ran from Kentucky?"

"Sophie. My life sucked. I mean it was awful. Your cabin is a dream come true compared to my trailer in Bentfork."

"Bentfork? There is actually a town named Bentfork?" Sophie threw her head back and howled. "That's perfect. Too, too perfect."

"Well it wasn't perfect. Wasn't perfect at all," Lorelei said as she shook more hot sauce on her eggs. She picked up a salty strip of bacon, dabbed a corner on the spicy sauce and took a bite. "Bentfork is a tiny town. Not much of anything there except misery and booze." She took another bite. "Hated it. But it was home. Didn't know much different."

"Your folks?"

"My mama died when I was little. Cancer. My daddy died over a year ago."

"Oh, I'm sorry Lorelei." She was truly sincere too.

"It's okay. My daddy was miserable. He's better off. Trust me. My mama though. That hurt." Her eyes became a bit distant as she spoke. "When she got sick, I mean real sick, my Aunt Adelaide stayed with us for a while." She looked across at Sophie. "That's how I got the bakery. She left it to me."

"She must have loved you very much."

"Never knew what that word meant until my aunt showed up." Lorelei shared a sorrowful smile with Sophie, and shrugged. "My folks—well. Let's just say they weren't the affectionate kind. They were hard. You know? But they fed us, taught us to hunt, bought us dog after dog after dog. Once mama got sick, well, I guess that's when things got bad. Daddy started drinking more and more. Couldn't get work. My aunt came down to help."

"People here still remember Adelaide. Seems like she was quite a character from what I hear. Though from local gossip, you're blowing her reputation away."

Lorelei smiled. "That's how I learned to bake. She taught me. It saved me too. That's what I did. Baked in the supermarket. Though people in town never developed a taste for wild mango spice muffins. They thought I was weird."

"And your brother?"

"Oh man. He's a mess. It's awful." Lorelei paused a moment. "Sophie, I can't go back ever. It's done." Her shoulders shook gently and she swiped a few tears from her eyes. "I can't." The tears were flowing freely.

"Hold it, hold it. What happened?" Sophie tossed her a napkin. "What do you mean you can't go back? That bakery is yours."

"Not anymore. It's his. I'm not doing it again. Ever."

"Doing what?" Sophie demanded. "Slow down." Sophie reached across the table and grabbed her hands, gently, connecting them both. "Now, tell me. You stole his money?"

"Sophie! My brother is a dealer. He sold drugs for years from our trailer. I knew one day he'd get caught, or arrested. Or worse. I bailed him outta more scraps than I can count. Fixed his car, paid his bills, loaned him money." She shook her head in disgust. "And all the while he had a mountain of cash hidden in the wall of the trailer. Thousands it looked like. Bastard."

"Ah, it's making sense now." She leaned back in her chair and processed the story.

"So. He was drunk. Passed out on the floor. He was making a deal or something I guess. Didn't hide it very well." She paused to think about her actions on that rainy night. "I saw the box sticking out of the wall. I thought it was rolls of some kind of green dynamite or something. May have been as well. Blew everything up anyway. So. I took it, well, half of it." She looked up at Sophie. "And then I left. Took his dog too. I wasn't planning to leave so soon. Or like that anyway."

She looked at Sophie whose smile was wide and sure.

"Why you smiling at me? What's so good about that? I'm as

big a crook as he is. Never spent a dime of his money though, but I'm just as dirty."

"You're no crook, Lorelei."

"Oh yeah I am."

"Well, you're sitting at my table and I don't serve crooks. I'm looking at someone very different from a crook."

Lorelei looked at Sophie. "Well. I sure feel like one. Dirty and used."

"Lorelei, enough of the pity. We'll work on that later. What I'm seeing is remarkable."

"Huh?"

"You heard me. Remarkable."

"Well, I sure don't feel remarkable. I've lost everything."

"Bullshit. The only thing you've lost is pride, and we can get that back. But right now? Sitting in front of me? You're no crook. You made a bad decision, sure. But that's one bad decision in a life of keeping you and your family afloat. How many hours a week did you work?"

"About fifty."

"And your brother?"

"Couldn't keep a job."

"Exactly."

"Sophie! I stole drug money and then threw it in his face. Right in his face! Chase was there. He heard everything. He's a cop."

Sophie took a breath and tried to regroup her thoughts. "Yeah. That sucks. We'll work on that too. But right now, let's get rid of this thief complex thing, okay?"

"It's not a complex. I stole money."

"Oh please, Lorelei! You're not Cat Woman! You didn't break into a jewelry store. You saw your brother's stash at helped yourself. Illegal stash I may add. Didn't you say you paid the bills? Bailed him out? For how long?"

"Years," she said.

"Seems to me you're a smart businesswoman. You saw your opportunity to get paid back and seized it. I would have done the same thing, but I wouldn't have stopped at half. There is interest you know."

Lorelei let that sink in.

"What am I going to do? I can't go back there. I'm not going back."

"What? You're just going to run away, again? Sneak out and then what? Go where?"

Lorelei sat silent.

"And Chase? What about him?"

Lorelei avoided Sophie's eyes. She knew Chase was a thorn between them both.

"You know, that day I came to your shop and bought all those orange muffin things? I actually came to tell you off."

"Huh?"

"That's right. I was going to show up, tell you off, then go on my way. I was jealous. I've known Chase for years, watched him nurse Fran through the day she died, watched him crumble at her service too. I could wait for him to come around. Guy like him, I'd wait a century. And I chose to wait too. Waited too long I guess."

Lorelei nudged a small nugget of scrambled egg around her plate, like a small pencil eraser, attempting to wipe away the conversation she knew should follow.

"Sophie, I—"

"Nope, no need kiddo. I've been playing the field too long and know when I've lost."

"I'm sorry. I didn't mean—"

"That's not the point. I came into your shop planning to tell you to back off. The grand 'that man is mine' thing." Sophie laughed a bit. It sounded so ridiculous in retrospect.

"So why didn't you?"

"I couldn't. From the moment I stepped into your shop, I don't know. Things shifted. I felt foolish and, well—shameful. So I just decided to make it look like I had a purpose, you know? Then you gave me a bite of that sponge cake and it took me back years. I swear. I nearly melted. Do you remember what you asked me?"

"What's it taste like? I do that for every—"

"No. Nope. This was different. I tried to play it off, but inside? Every hug my mother ever gave me was wrapping their arms around me all over again. It was like I couldn't breath. Here I was, in your pretty girly shop, and all I could think of was my mother and wanted to hug her again." Sophie paused. "I had to get out."

"But Sophie. You didn't just leave. You bought almost every cupcake. I thought there was a party I didn't know about."

Sophie laughed. "Oh! There was a party all right. Boy was there a party! What the hell did you put into those cupcakes? Some of your brother's secret spice?"

"What?"

"I took those muffins to the retirement center where my mom lived and handed them out. Seems like all hell broke loose that day and it wasn't just the sugar!"

"What are you talking about?"

"Tucker? The guy with the tow truck? He works there and told me quite a few stories last night. While you were in LaLa land, we sat outside on the porch and wow!" she said with a raised brow.

"What? Did people get sick?" she asked concerned.

"Sick? Ha! Sick nothing, those folks were bed swapping all day and night! From the stories he told me, the Fordhook Home for the elderly made *50 Shades of Grey* look like a church lunch!"

"What?"

Sophie laughed. "Dancing in the halls, naked! Couples on the bocci ball court, *on* the court. You hear me? Communal showers, and showering was not the prime objective I hear. Sounds like it was quite a time."

"Oh my—"

"Seems like they really loved your mango-spiced-latte-chi-whatever-the-hell-it-was cupcakes."

"Sophie— I didn't—"

"And you know what else?" She paused a moment, and said softly, "My mom passed away that day. She, um—she died." Sophie stared into her coffee for a moment then greeted Lorelei with a sincere smile. "She gave me something though. Something wonderful and I think—"

"Oh my gosh. Sophie. I'm so sorry— I—"

"Not a word. We'll talk about this later." She stood up and ended the conversation. "I'm taking a shower and off to work. You get cleaned up and figure out a way to clean up your mess.

We'll talk more at dinner. Okay? Wait a minute. What's this?"

Sophie leaned forward and picked something from Lorelei's disheveled hair.

A small white flower.

Lorelei gulped.

"You have a flower stuck in your hair. Figures, of course Doris Day sprouts flowers every morning. Sure she does. Just like all of us," she said with a sarcastic edge and ran upstairs to the shower.

"I am not Doris Day! I'm a rotten crook and I'm dangerous!" She yelled after Sophie. She heard the bathroom door shut in a recessed hallway above. She shifted her eyes to the delicate white flower on the table, nearly lost among dirty breakfast plates and crumpled napkins.

She picked up a dirty plate and walking to the sink, did her best to wipe away the tears that were forming in her eyes. The gasps came quickly and she abandoned herself to a silent sob of heartbreak.

With a sloppy, heavy tongue, Waffles licked the plate clean.

Chapter 18

Three days later, Sophie sat in her car outside Thoreau's Pub. She auto dialed her cell.

"Cobweb Corners Police Department, Officer Chase Harris speaking. Is this an emergency?"

"Yes, it's an emergency. If you don't get Little Mary Sunshine outta my house you're going to have one hell of a clean up on your hands! I'm talking *man down* kinda mess."

Chase laughed. "Hey Sophie! What's going on?"

"Your Miss Sunshine, Lorelei, has been staying with me for three days and she's driving me and my dog crazy! She's a sweet kid, but I'm warning you, I want her out!"

"Wait a minute, wait a minute. Lorelei is living with you? Holy hell. I've been worried sick."

"She got her car hung up in a ditch on Route 12. Tucker gave her a tow to my place, and she's been there since. Can't get her out. Now I don't know what going on between you and—"

"Sophie, you know this call is being recorded, right? How about I meet you at the pub. My shift's over at 3:00."

"You're on, and you better bring back up!"

By the time Sophie handed Chase his order of fried fish and chips, the lunch crowd was winding down and only few tables remained. A couple of stragglers sat at the bar watching the game, punctuating the air with unified supportive cheers and occasional groans of disappointment.

Sophie removed her apron, balled it up, and tossed it in the corner of the booth. She slid across from Chase and grabbed a potato wedge the size of a fat, chewy thumb. "Chase, She's driving me crazy. I feel for her and all, but this kid has got to face the music."

She dipped the fry into some mayo. Pointing it like a sword, it became a weapon, a mayo tipped pointer used to accentuate her determination. "And let me tell you something, Caretaker for the broken-hearted club I am not! She even tried one of my cigarettes and lost her lunch all over the road. That kid sucks at slumming it. Now you get over there and have a talk with her."

"Not a chance. I'm done. Can't do it, Soph. Won't do it. I don't know what she told you but it's over. Her brother—"

"I know, I know. She told me all about it. For three days! Did I mention that she's been in the house for three days? It's like living with a psycho. One minute she's Betty Crocker, the next, she's ready for Betty Ford. And when she cries, she looks like an orphaned muppet. I'm done. Gimme another fry, I'm starved." She helped herself to his plate.

Chase leaned back in the booth, sighing in frustration. The conversation was going to be more difficult than he had imagined and he began looking for an escape route. "Soph, go easy on her—"

"Easy? I did! I helped her, gave her my couch, gave her my ear. Hell, even gave her my dog for two nights in a row. And let me tell you something Mr. Officer Man—" Another fry was dipped and jabbed at Chase's face. "Waffles doesn't sleep with anyone but me."

"Didn't know you had such a heart, Soph," he said with a wink.

"She's a sweetheart, but I'm too old for another slumber party. Come get her and talk some sense into that kid. She needs to get her life back. Get her back in that whacky bakery."

"You know I can't do that. I told you. I'm done. I don't want to get involved. Too much family mess going on there." He shifted his eyes away, leaned his head back, and took a long, pleasing pull from his beer.

She saw through the guise. "Chase, put all that BS aside.

You need to listen to her. Give her that much will you? You know I'm not crazy about her, but there's something there. Something good. Don't blow it. I don't know what it is, but in her own weird way, she's a fighter."

"Just like you," he laughed.

She immediately became defensive. "Not like me at all." She twirled a fat fry on the side of his plate. She thought for a moment, and then added with distant sincerity, "Well in a way she is I guess. Maybe you're right."

"Miss, can we get our check?" a young businessman interrupted her.

"Take it up to the bar, I'm talkin' here!" She shouted back, adding a wink and a nudge to the bartender. She looked back at Chase. His head was tilted back, resting against the red leatherette booth and his eyes were lost somewhere in the ancient rafters overhead. He looked exhausted. Resigned even.

She spoke. "Chase, the poor kid is sunk over you. I'm talking head over heels."

"Sophie, don't."

"Don't what? Don't tell you? Ignore it? You can't ignore it Chase. Its too late. It's already a part of you. You can't escape that."

"Sophie please. I'm telling you."

"Telling me what? You're telling me nothing. I see the way you look at her. It was evident the first time I met her, poor kid, and if I can't have a handsome guy like you, someone should. May as well be her. 'Bout time too! You copy?"

Chase furrowed his eyes a bit, feigning misunderstanding.

"I tried Chase. I really did," she smiled half-heartedly, fingering the remaining fries on his plate. "Figured if I waited long enough, you'd be ready for me."

The two looked across the table at each other and neither spoke. She cracked a half smile. "But now? Buddy, I see I'm not ready for you. Funny isn't it?" She toyed with a paper napkin. "I'm sorry you know grief the way you do. And now that mom passed, I see how it can make someone, I don't know—turn inside? Shut down I guess?" She looked up at him to see if he was following. The reflection in his warm brown eyes told her he was with her for every word. "There was a time when

I though maybe I could help heal you. I fell hard buddy." She smiled broadly and looked him in the eyes. Her sincere words were hitting home. "I thought I could get you to fall for me too." She shook her head a bit. "I thought I could take away your sadness at least. I don't know—I think it's something different now."

She warmed when she saw the bittersweet glow on Chase's warm mouth. She tried to find words she never knew how to express before. "I guess it's like that damn path in the Frost poem? About that guy and those two roads in the woods?" She smiled as she remembered. "I always hated that poem but it was drilled into us every freaking year in high school. I used to want to shout, 'Oh for God's sake! Take a cab!'"

Chase tossed back his head and let out a hearty laugh. Every kid in New England was raised on that poem and knew it by heart. He took another long pull from his beer. "I guess it means we're alone with that choice," he said with a shrug.

"No, it doesn't," she countered quickly. "It doesn't mean that at all. He's standing in front of two choices. One, he knows well. The same old same old. Safe and easy. The other is overgrown, wasn't it? Right? Kinda trashy? " She knitted her brow a bit trying to remember the line. "Or it wasn't used a lot, something like that. Anyway! The point is, he didn't take the path he knew."

Chase looked at his beer. He picked a corner of the damp label and said quietly, "And I took the one less traveled, and it made all the difference."

They held each other's eyes. Silent and knowing.

Sophie smiled. "Less traveled. Listen to you Mr. Poetry Man!"

The two smiled at each other, in silent recognition of something much deeper than the simple poem.

"Hey, Sophie," the bartender shouted. "Table three needs refills."

"What? You don't have legs?" she shouted back. "My shift's over." She turned her attention back to Chase whose eyes seemed lost in Frost's woods.

"Chase," she said softly, "you've been on the same road for a long time. Fran's road. You know? It's a beauty. Now, make a turn. Try it. That kid is waiting."

"It's harder than that, Soph."

"Who are you talkin' to? I know hard Chase! And I know loneliness. It sucks. But you've been on that same road so long you don't even recognize the scenery."

"What are you talking about? I take risks! I went out with Lorelei a few times! It's not like I'm sacred, Soph."

She stared at him, droll and smirking. "Really?"

"Besides," he added, leaning in for a bit of privacy, "there's stuff in that family I don't want to know about. Her brother—" He shook his head in disbelief. "You know she lied about that right? She has a brother. A twin brother! He's a dealer. Drug dealer. Before I heard anymore incriminating evidence. I took off."

"The same road. I get it."

"What? No. I'm a cop, Sophie! I—"

"All right, officer, listen to me. I was in love with you, got it?" She was suddenly direct. And though confrontational, the sincerity in her voice took center stage. "I know it's not ever going to pan out. I see that. You're a great guy but man are you blowing it. There is a woman in my house who is head over heels in love with you Chase, and from what I see under your tough guy uniform, you fell for her as well. I've got nothing to gain here. You only got an inch of her story. Her story, hear me? You took off before you could hear any more. You get to write the rest of the story all by yourself on that same old road through the woods. Easy isn't it?"

"I heard enough."

"Still on that road, huh? Refuse to budge? You're blowing it buddy."

"Sophie, stop. Isn't it enough that I lost—"

"Chase! Loss is everywhere! You know that better than anybody! Your road is not *loss*! My road is not being alone for ever! I know that now. But if we don't shift gears, that's how our stories will be written. And she took the road she always traveled and ended up in a dirty house coat with fifty cats!"

Chase laughed.

"That's not going to be me. And I suggest the same for you. You knew a love that I never had. Maybe that's why I fell for you. Who knows. I wanted some of that. It looked really good." She looked into his eyes and smiled sincerely as she saw him blush a little. She was stunned being so genuine with him was this easy. "You have the chance again. What are you waiting for?"

He shrugged, picked at the label some more. "She's not like other people," he said.

"Don't I know it! But Chase, that's exactly the point. She's the road less traveled. Don't you see it?"

"But there's more Sophie. She has this thing—"

"Chase. I love you. This bar loves you. This town loves you. And yes, Fran loved you. But that is past tense. I don't care what you decide to do about Lorelei. But you have to at least talk to her. Listen to her then decide which road you're choosing. Don't waste it."

"I get it."

"Good," she said, grabbing her balled up apron. "Now, I'm outta here. You're a great guy. I wish you knew that, too."

She was half way across the bar when Chase called out to her. "Hey, Sophie!"

"Yeah?" She whirled around and caught his shining eyes.

"Thanks. I mean, well—thanks."

"Anytime, Officer Harris. You're my hero. You know that." She gave him one last wink and was out the front door.

Twilight was falling over the town, casting the parking lot and Thoreau's Pub in a soft amber glow. She stood alone and smiled into the afternoon sun. For the first moment in a long time, she felt strangely at peace.

Chapter 19

Sophie pulled into the driveway, and stamping out her cigarette in the overflowing ashtray, reminded herself to be firm but encouraging with Lorelei. She rehearsed her speech over and over on the ride home. Her talk with Chase reminded her that she needed to get her own life on track. Her mother's passing, the arrangements and estate, the funeral. It was all over, finished with a nice clean ribbon and the town's blessing, but still, it exhausted her. Time to open some windows, let some light and air in! Maybe even quit smoking, join a book club. Something.

Either way, Lorelei had to go.

Tonight.

As she approach the cabin, she heard Waffles and his usual barking routine. She smiled slightly. In the past his incessant barking was annoying and a bother. But tonight? There was something different in his tone. It was welcoming. His voice told her that she was expected and someone was thrilled for her arrival. "Crazy mutt" she mumbled and walked inside.

The aroma hit her instantly and she froze, keys dangling like dead weigh in her fingertips.

Coconut and banana? Banana bread was it? And lemon, there was definitely a crisp hint of lemon … and cream? Creamy lemon curd? How can all these flavors sing in such harmony together? But they did. In perfect tune. As she stood, inhaling the aroma surrounding her, a new note arrived, singing softly in the background like a lullaby, a warm spice that filled her lungs and nearly made her weep with comfort.

The moment shattered and Waffles was upon her. Paws on

her chest, tongue slurping and fat tail wagging like a sped up, drunken metronome.

Sophie soaked it in. Who cares if it was an old mutt. It was love and she received his welcome as though she were a queen.

She took a final deep breath and held it in her lungs. This is perfect she thought. Right here, right now, perfect.

"Welcome home, Sophie!" the cheery voice called. "I made you a surprise as a thank you gift."

Oh God please stop talking — just stop talking and let me soak this in ...

She opened her eyes. "Well, June Cleaver! Don't you look like a ray of sunshine!" She turns her attention to the dog and covered him in kisses. "Yes yes yes Waffles. Who's mommy's good boy? Who's mommy's boy?"

"That dog sure does love you."

"Happy somebody does," she replied and tossed her purse on the table. Exhausted, she walked to the kitchen to grab a beer.

"Why do you say it like that?" Lorelei asked.

"Like what? Just an observation. That's all. Glad my dog loves me. I am so glad my dog loves me!"

"Sounds like you had a hard day."

"No. A hard life. But my dog loves me!" Came the sarcastic reply from the kitchen.

"You know who you remind me of?" Lorelei asked.

"No. Who?"

"You ever read *Gone with the Wind*?"

"Nope," she answered flatly as she popped open the beer.

"Well, there's this character, Belle Watling. You remind me of her."

"That's so? What's this Belle all about. The belle of the ball?"

"Oh no. Nothing like that." Lorelei laughed. "She's the town whore and she's this incredible—"

She stopped talking the moment she saw Sophie's face peer around the wall.

"The town whore? The town whore? I remind you of the town whore?"

"Oh my gosh no! I didn't mean it like that at all! I mean

she's really um—"

"Go on. This better be good," Sophie's tone dripped sarcasm thicker than oil.

"Well okay, yes, she is the town whore, well Madame really. But she's like the strongest character in the book. She's, well, she's like you that way."

"I'm a strong whore?"

"No! Will you listen? I didn't mean it like that. And you know what? So what if I did? You're always calling me Nancy Drew and Doris Day and June Cleaver! And I'm hardly a goody goody except to you! So, I didn't say you were the town whore. I said you reminded me of one. There's a difference."

Sophie laughed and tossed herself on the couch. "Touché. Okay. I'll take that. So, tell me about this Belle." She settled in to hear the story.

"She's like the only independent woman in the book. Sure, Scarlett is strong, but she relies so heavily on men that she still, well, loses I guess."

"Kiddo, I have news for you. Prostitutes are completely dependent upon men, too."

Lorelei sighed. "I know, I know. But Belle is different. She lives her life the way she wants to and makes sure that the ladies who work for her are taken care of I guess. She doesn't care what other people think. All the other ladies in the book live under this awful microscope. They're so scared of what people think about them. But not Belle. She doesn't care what other people say."

Sophie decided she wouldn't join a book group after all. Frost and *Gone with the Wind* all in one day was just too much.

"That's why you remind me of Belle. You're strong like that too."

"Thanks, I guess."

"Even when the war comes. She doesn't run away. She stays and fights I think. It's funny though." She furrowed her brows. "I can't remember whose side she's on."

"Hun, that sounds more like you than it does me."

"What?"

"Whose side are you on, Lorelei?"

"What does that mean?"

"It means that you have a pretty big battle ahead, and you've already set yourself up to lose."

"What? Where are you going? I'm talking about Belle! And my battle is long over."

"Your brother?" she said with a raised brow. "You began your life here with a lie— and believe me, I understand that! Really. But kiddo, you're making the battle worse."

"No I'm not, I'm ending it. Already have."

"You said you liked Belle because she stayed and fought."

"I know," she said with a hint of defeat in her voice.

"You also couldn't remember what side she was on. Kiddo, I never even read the book, and even I can see what's behind that."

"I made some cupcakes—"

"Oh no you don't. You are not deflecting this talk to your whacky cakes."

"I'm not—"

"Listen to me. I'm done here, okay? I need my life back, and you are done retreating. The vacation is over. You need to toughen up sister. I don't care what you do, but you owe Chase an explanation." She raised a brow and took a quick gulp of her beer.

"But I—"

"No. Your turn to be the town harlot. Really! Toughen up. Stop running away and lying about your past! Talk with Chase, work it out or end it. I don't care. But let me warn you. He's been through enough. Got it?"

"I got it." She thought for a pained moment. "This is hard Sophie. I think I hurt him real bad. I never meant to."

"Well you did, and now you brought a druggie into the mix as well. This is a bad combination. Anything else in that book of yours that can help us?"

"Well one character says 'tomorrow is another day.' Maybe that's good advice."

Sophie exploded in a hard laugh. "That's the biggest line of bullshit I ever heard. 'Tomorrow is another day?' Holy Crap!" She howled. "Of course it is! Now listen to me. You can return to Kentucky or you can reclaim your bakery. I don't care. But you can't leave without tying up your loose ends. Got it?"

"I got it. You're hard Sophie."

"Don't I know it!"

"I guess I start with home. That means Beeker." She thought for a moment, brow furrowing in deep confusion. "Yes?"

"Sounds good. What are you thinking?"

"I can't let him live here Sophie. I took a ton of his money. Never spent a dime of it though. Threw it back in his face too. Hopefully he took off, probably took Bear."

"If he got what he wanted, he's probably long gone by now. Problem number one is solved. Good riddance."

Lorelei took a deep breath. "And then Chase. If he'll talk to me."

"He might. What would Belle do?"

"Belle would, well— she'd confront him I guess. Not a lot of words, but she'd get the point out. Oh boy. This is going to hurt."

Waffles settled his head onto Sophie's lap. "Yes. It will. But, it's what happens when we sign up." She gave Waffles a hearty head rub.

"Huh? Sign up for what?"

"Sign up for love." She held Lorelei's fearful eyes for a long time.

"I didn't say anything about that," Lorelei whispered.

"No. I did." She pulled the dog in closely and rubbed his floppy ears. "For the first time since he lost Fran, I saw him smile. I mean really smile. And it was directed right at you. He fell for you. You ran away. Now fix it."

Sophie was direct, but kind, and Lorelei understood.

"I made you some cupcakes, as a thank you. I guess I really mean it now."

"Smelled them the minute I walked in. What are you waiting for? Bring 'em on!"

"Don't think they'd go well with beer. Can I get you a glass of milk?"

Sophie rolled her eyes, but played along. "Milk and cookies, how sweet."

"Cupcakes, not cookies. I made cupcakes."

"I hope they taste like mentholated filter tips! I could go for a pack right now," Sophie joked, but when she saw the cupcakes presented before her, the joking stopped and words froze in her throat.

On her mother's old Blue Willow cake plate were six of the most artful and dazzling cupcakes she had ever seen. Intricate lavender pansies were set upon a brilliant downy-yellow icing, softer than the quietest sunrise.

Sophie stared, breathless, in silent shock, for rising in the center of each cupcake was a brilliant orange butterfly. Six beautiful butterflies and a dozen wings of fire orange and golden yellow, glistening like church windows, delicate as angel's breath.

"The butterflies—" she whispered as she remembered the day her mother passed away, the window covered with a thousand beating butterfly wings set against a setting sun. "How did you—"

"They're just so pretty," Lorelei said. "I spent all afternoon on the wings. I just thought you'd—"

"Lorelei," Sophie said with a smile wider than the ocean itself, "Where did you come from?"

"Huh?"

"Give me one of those. I have to see someone."

"What?"

"I've decided to take my own advice," she said as she grabbed a cupcake, her purse, and was out the door. "Leave the key under the mat when you leave," she hollered over her shoulder.

"Sophie wait! Where are you going?"

"Kiddo, I've been playing the town strumpet all wrong. Does Belle have a lot of customers?"

"Huh? Well, yes. Kinda, yes."

"See? Nobody knocking at my door. I've been chasing them all away."

"But—"

"No buts!" She stopped and looked at the confused young lady in the doorway. "Lorelei, we couldn't be any different, you and I. But you taught me something. You really did."

It felt good to say that.

"Where are you going?"

"Well, there's this road I forgot all about. Time to see where it goes!"

Chapter 20

When Sophie pulled into the parking lot of Fordhook's Home, she saw Tucker walking toward his car.

"Tucker!" she called. "Hey, Tucker!"

"Hey, Soph! How's it going?" he said as he approached. Even from a distance, she melted at the way his faded jeans jacket gripped his solid shoulders. "Your mom's service was real nice. You did her proud."

Sophie broke eye contact for a moment. It was the last thing on her mind. "Thanks," she said. "It was nice, wasn't it?" She folded her arms in front of her chest and patted her elbows awkwardly, unsure how to begin.

"What are you doing here?" he asked.

Sophie took a deep breath and channeling her inner Belle, she began. "Tucker, I hope you'll forgive me, but I want to tell you something and I don't know where to begin." Her words were rushed and came in rapid fire succession. "So if you have a minute, can you talk? I really need to talk to you because there is this —"

"Hold it hold it, slow down," he laughed. What's going on? You need a lift somewhere?"

She took a deep breath. "A lift? Yes, I need a lift!" She laughed. She looked into his warm eyes and saw a smiling man looking back. His brows arched wonderingly. And though his defined shoulders and chiseled jaw nearly melted her, it was the upturned lips and scruffy cheeks that slid into a beaming smile that did her in.

"You take my breath away."

"Um. What?" he said.

"You heard me, and I don't care what you think, or don't think," she said joyfully. "I don't care!" She was breathless in her release. "Every week when I came to see my mama in here, you were the reason I could leave smiling. Your face, your kindnesses to me and my mama, even the way you'd ask me how I was made me feel like I was someone who mattered. And your God-forgive-me gorgeous face! So. There it is." She shrugged, embarrassed and fulfilled.

"Sophie. I don't know what to say."

"Oh God, you're not gay, are you?"

"What?" he laughed. "No, no, I'm not gay." He shook his head smiling all the while.

"Girlfriend?"

"No. No girlfriend," he said. His smile, flirtatious and welcoming encouraged Sophie.

"Not on the market?" She asked bluntly.

"No, no. I'm definitely on the market," he said, folding his arms and leaning against her car, smiling broadly.

"Well then? I am here for an official announcement," she said. "Tucker, you are the hottest thing on two feet, and you've been charming me for years, and if you don't go out to dinner with me tonight, I'll lose my faith in humanity, America, and every fairy tale ever written."

Tucker laughed, truly enjoying her proposition.

"Well, if it means all that how can I say no? You're on. Where are you taking me?"

She lit up. "I know this great little spot on the beach. Under the old lighthouse. They serve the best clams ever. Nice fire pit too. A little breezy though."

"Sophie, you are something else," he laughed. "You're asking me out on a date?"

"I am."

Smiling broadly, he said "Sounds great to me."

She smiled in relief. It was happening, and somewhere within her protected heart, a small light began to grow. "Wait a minute. I got you something," she said and reached into her car for Lorelei's cupcake.

"Wow! That's incredible," he said, gazing upon remarkable cupcake in her hands. "I thought the last batch was amazing.

But this? Can you actually eat it?"

"Of course you can! Lorelei made them today, so I brought one for you."

"Butterfly too. Very cool. And all this time I didn't think you even knew my last name."

"What?" She said.

"My last name," he said with a handsome grin.

She laughed, embarrassed. "You're right," she said. "I just know you as Tucker. I even have you in my contacts that way. Just Tucker." She shrugged.

"Sophie," he said with a grin, "my last name is Monarch."

"Oh," she said deeply, holding his inviting eyes, "Oh, this is good. This is really good." She was practically purring.

As she handed him the cupcake, their hands met, and Lorelei's innocent charm began. The butterfly, in all of its delicate sugar and glaze, began to move. Subtly at first, it took a few small beats like the breath of a newborn and was soon airborne. Free of the sweet grounding that held it back, it lifted gently into the air. Dancing in the twilight, its wings beat in rhythm with the heartbeats of the new found lovers. It fluttered between them, fanning their hearts, and without magic or guile, was soon lost in the twilight stars above them.

They never even saw its flight. Their eyes only saw the magic and grace of the lover's eyes sparkling before them.

Miles above the butterfly's graceful flight, a small woman sat in the window seat of a 747 bound for Paris, and she wasn't frightened. As the plane whizzed across the night sky, she looked upon the beautiful earth beneath her and nearly wept with joy. It was all so beautiful down there. A spinning blue marble of wonder and delicacy, she was grateful to finally reach this view. Tori held the Paris guide book in her hands and whispered to no one in particular, "Thank you." She closed her eyes for a moment, and wished for grace upon all of the earthbound inhabitants below. Her smile was particularly broad that evening.

As the plane soared into the twilight air across the Eastern seaboard, Tori took one last glance at the dimming earth below, land and sea. Had she magical powers, her eyes may have landed upon a middle aged man, surfing through the Autumn waves. He was shouting a song he had long forgotten— a song of love regained and he knew he would not live his life alone any longer. His heart opened abundantly that night as his toes clutched the wet board that flew through the watery world beneath him.

Further inland (had Tori the magical sight required for such visions), she would have seen a particular home in the center of her town, quietly transforming throughout the night into a bower of roses, nearly drowning the sleeping occupant with the delicate fragrance of her mother's garden.

And inside that cottage? Grace Ogden slept deeply the night the vines grew tall, squeezing and scrunching their way from the fertile soil surrounding her bungalow. They reached their tendrils above window-sills and doors, thorns clung to shutter and shingle, and buds grew abundantly, exploding their memories of perfume and romance into the morning air of Cobweb Corners.

Grace awoke that morning in a slight haze. Confused and sleepy, she shook the cobwebs from her mind and tried to focus. Her bedroom, dim and shadowed, made her believe it was still night, but the light was different somehow, diffused. Green and mysterious, liquid almost, it spread its thorny shadowed tendrils along her oaken floor and led her eyes to the window where she politely gasped.

Rose tendrils, fat as a giantess's thumb, twisted their way across her bedroom window and only allowed the bravest emerald light to reach inside. Sunlight diamonds twinkled upon lush, green leaves as tiny pink buds winked their bliss at her in wonderful surprise.

She lifted her shaking fingers to her mouth.

"Oh my—"

It was barely a whisper.

Voices on her front lawn quickly took her attention. Rushing away from the window, she grabbed her robe and headed to the front door.

The same fecund green shadows haunted the silent living

room and filled the space with an underwater glow, mystic and growing.

She tentatively approached the front door, and the cacophony of voices outside grew. Indistinguishable and choral, they rose and fell with *ohs* and *ahs* like the audience of a spectacular fireworks display.

Shy and wary, she slowly opened the heavy door.

Like Briar Rose waking from a hundred years sleep, she was not surprised to see the wall of blossom, thorn, and leaf, blocking her way. A prison of green.

Even Mary Lennox feared the discovery of her secret garden. Transformations can be threatening.

"Judy?" she called politely. "Are you out there? I can't see a thing!"

"Grace? Is that you?" a disembodied voice in the crowd replied.

"Of course it's me! Who else would it be? What's happening?"

"Grace! Stay where you are. The roses are growing."

The crowd gasped in unison as another hundred blossoms unfurled in the morning light.

Grace was not afraid. If something was going on in her lawn, she wanted to see it. Clutching her robe tightly around her waist, she reached out and shook a thick rose stalk. It gently released its hold and other vines took notice. No fear of thorn or spike, Grace gently stepped through the fragrant jungle and emerged, slightly disheveled, but whole.

Embarrassed by the large crowd gathered on her front lawn, she tried to gently fix her bed head and noticed the crowd was growing and spilling into the street.

"Grace, look!" Judy was by her side in an instant. "They've been growing like this all morning."

Grace stepped back a few feet in order to take it all in.

It was astonishing.

Where her bungalow once sat was now a forest of abundant roses. Clutching the chimney and embracing the home in their luxurious growth, door, window and roof became one with vine, foliage, and bud.

The crowd watched in awe as another hundred buds

flickered pink, grew engorged and ripe, then opened their petals in obscene delight to reveal trousseaus of fragrance and stamen.

"I like it," she said with an air of delighted defiance. "I think I'll keep it."

Chapter 21

The scent of roses was strong that morning and drifted across Cobweb Corners like a gentle breath of intoxicating perfume. Lorelei sat in her Bug across the street from her house. She hoped she'd find the house and bakery empty, no sign of the confrontation four days before, no drug money on the floor, no Beeker, and what of Bear? Probably gone too.

No such luck.

She sat in the car and stared at Beeker who sat on the front porch, staring back, Bear sleeping at his feet.

"Bastard," she mumbled, wishing he'd look more out of place on their aunt's porch, her porch.

Trouble is, he didn't look out of place at all. Looked like he'd even found a home, and that's what made her take action.

She got out of the car, resisted slamming the door too hard, and made her way across the empty street. She stood in the front of the bakery, arms folded and simply glared at Beeker who was leaning back in his old chair, balancing it on its two rear legs.

"Well?" He said. "What took you?"

"I came to get my house back."

"Figured," he said.

"I want you gone. You got your money, now go." She tried to keep it easy and direct.

"I want m'dog too," he said simply.

She paused a moment and stared at him. Was he really that thick? "Beeker, you never cared one lick for that old hound. Living under the trailer like that, it's a wonder he lasted this long. Take him. Go! I don't care. Just go."

Beeker set his chair gently on the porch and looked at his sister, one brow raised and the edge of his mouth turned up in a hurtful smile.

"What are you so mad at Lorelei?" He asked. She ignored the hint of sincerity in his voice. "Hell, it was my money you stole. My dog you stole. Never even said goodbye."

"What?" she said. "Boy, you were passed out drunk on the floor. You got a lot of nerve tracking me here." Beeker turned his head away, avoiding her accusing eyes. "I carried you for too long and now that I have my own life, you can't have any part of it. You hear me? I want you gone, Beeker!"

A loose shutter on an upper window banged a gentle retort, demanding their attention for a moment. The twins stood in silent submission: one on the porch, too scared to speak, one on the earth, too frightened to move.

"Well?" she asked.

"Well what?" He mumbled.

"Get moving. Get offa my porch and get outta my life."

"Why are you so mad Lala? What happened?"

"Mad? Why am I so mad?" And then her fury opened. She released it, out, over the lawn, up the porch stairs where it slammed into Beeker's lap. Like a long overdue storm, it soaked the receiver to the bone. "From the first day we were born I've been carrying you around, feeding you, washing you when mama couldn't, reading you stories when their fights got so bad it shook the trailer like lightening! Mad? Hell yes I'm mad!" and she shook like the thunder. "And what did I get from it? Huh? Since when did you ever try lifting a finger to help unless it was to drain another bottle of Jack down your miserable throat!"

"Lala, stop," he whispered.

"And what? What did it get me? Nothing but creeps shouting in the night for your stash of drugs. I'm working my ass off at that lousy supermarket while you do nothing but drink, smoke, gamble with your life. My life. Our lives, Beeker! Our lives mean more than that. And what are you going to do? Huh? Just go home to that awful trailer in the woods and smoke your weed till you just disappear? Lord I hope so! Just disappear Beeker!" She laughed at the image. Like a second rate magic show, a puff of fake smoke, and he's gone. Poof!

"You show up here and ruined everything! My one shot at happiness! Real, honest to goodness happiness is gone because of you! Something really great! And now I lost him because of you! You hear me?" Her fury grew. "You listening to me? I'll never get that back. Now get off my porch and disappear. I hate you!"

Gasps of breath stuck in her heaving throat. Too angry to even look at the disheveled young man on the porch, she wiped her arm across her mouth, wet from spittle and angry shouting.

She took a final breath, ready to begin again when she saw Beeker's face. Though his expression remained sturdy, he couldn't hide the tears on his cheeks.

"Never seen you so angry before," he managed, wiping a dirty sleeve across his face.

"Don't. Talk," she uttered through gritted teeth.

"Can I just tell you something?"

"Beeker! Enough."

"I'm clean, Lorelei. Gave it all up the night you left." It was out. Simple, easy, and quiet. "Even went to AA."

She stared at him, arms folded protectively in front of her. "Uh huh," she said.

"Haven't had a lick of anything. Won't either."

Lorelei broke eye contact and looked into the distance. The waves continued to pound their ethereal rhythm, lulling the universe into their gentle arms, which seemed so many miles away. Lorelei spoke.

"And?"

"And what?"

"You're clean. Good, Beeker. Good for you." She refused to offer any more than that.

"Never got into any hard stuff anyway," he added. "I just did it for the money, trying to get by as best as I could."

"That's a laugh! Beeker, you're killing me." She shook her head in disbelief.

"Huh?" he asked, half a lip in an upturned questioning snarl.

"All that time you had a bank full of cash hidden in the

trailer. Beeker! You lied to me, cheated me, put us both at risk. You're an ass Beeker."

"What could I do Lorelei? Huh? Give it away? Give it to you and say 'Here! All better now! Let's go buy a house.'"

"Pay your own damn bills for one thing. That's what you could have done!"

He stared at her. She was right.

"Sorry," he added, shame creeping into his voice.

"Sorry? Do you even hear yourself?"

"Yeah I do," he confronted. "I screwed up! But I'll tell you this. I sound a lot better than you do."

"What?" She approached the porch stairs and grabbed the old railing for support.

"I do! You're so lost in anger it's made you ugly! Never seen you so pissed before. Guess I deserve it. But Lorelei, I came here to apologize. Finally got my car reliable enough to make this awful trip. Figured you spent all that money fixing this place up. Hell! I don't even want the dog. You keep him. I came here to apologize."

"Okay," she said softly. "I got it."

"Wasn't till I got here that I learned you totally wrote me out of your life. Your buddy there didn't even know you had a brother. You lied? About me?"

She looked him squarely in the eye. "Had to. Hoped to forget all about you and that dirty trailer. Tried real hard to bury you too." It hurt to say it. She was shocked when she heard the words that formed on her lips. The awful choking lump grew in her throat, blocking her words and breath, barely allowing her to speak. "I had to," she whispered. "I had to bury you, Daddy, Mama, the whole awful thing— just so I could get by."

Beeker was right. She did sound ugly. Real ugly.

"Lorelei. I don't want that money. It's yours. I don't want Bear. Keep him. I don't want anything from you. I just came to apologize. You're the only family left. Figured you should know."

"Yeah, thanks," she whispered.

"I'm sorry, La. I am. Can't run from each other too long. It's like I'm drowning all over again and I hate it."

"Don't drown," she said softly.

"Got nothing left."

And even more softly than before, "Don't drown. Don't." It became a whisper.

When Lorelei walked toward her brother that morning, it was a journey twenty-six years in the making. Finally empty of rancor and blame, she took a few steps toward the crying man in the chair.

"Stand up," she said.

He looked up at her, and though his man's face revealed a life of hardship and battles, his eyes revealed the fears of a young boy, standing on the edge of the world.

"I got nuthin'. There's nothing left." He didn't move.

"Don't drown," she said again, and as she felt the tears run from her clear eyes, she knew they were open and ready to finally see the world and her life in it.

"I'm sorry, La," he said again, choking silently on his words, elbows on his knees, staring deeply into the floor, wishing he were miles below the old wooden floor that held him in the light.

"Look at me?" she asked him.

"Can't."

"Beeker, look at me?"

When she saw his eyes, she knew the fights and pains of their twenty-six years together had been washed away, revealing an authentic iris that only honesty knows. Clear and blue, insightful as a thousand sunrises and mysterious as a silver moon beam, Lorelei knew she was looking into sincerity itself.

And from her view, it looked okay.

In fact, it looked pretty good.

It really did.

So, she smiled.

Later that night when dinner was done and tomorrow's cakes were baking, he swept the floor and she made icing. He washed the dishes, and she whipped some cream. He filled pastry bags, and she showed him how to make roses. He licked a spoon, and she licked a spatula. They smiled softly and working in harmony, hummed tunes from long ago and got to work.

"What about the money?" she asked gently. "I don't want it. It's like rat poison."

"I don't want it either. I have an idea though," he said simply, a twinkle in his eye.

As she listened to Beeker's idea, she raised a brow and a corner of her mouth in a mischievous smile. She was loving this.

"That's it, Beeker," she whispered with ease, loving the perfect poetry of his plan. His relief shown through, and her smile took wing that night, illuminating the stars that lit their small corner of the world.

If you happened to be driving through Cobweb Corners that night, would you have thought it odd if an old VW bug made a few unplanned stops at random mailboxes? Would you have been concerned when an arm reached out into the dark night, opened the unknown recipient's box, and tossed a random object inside?

Would you have laughed to hear the muffled cheer rise from the Bug's interior as brother and sister sped away?

Or, would you follow them on their midnight flight through town. Another mailbox, another joyful cheer. A library book return box, an animal shelter donation crate, the elementary school and fire department, hair salon and diner, all received the same wadded up cylinder of mysterious cash that night, held by a simple tan rubber band.

But what if their journey took you all the way to the end of town, up Old Newport road, passed the bakery to the abandoned lighthouse and old pier? Would you turn around then? Or captivated by the celebration in front of you, would you watch the pair exit their car, and walk to the end of the pier?

That's what Chase did. He sat in his car under the shadow

of the lighthouse and watched as two figures walked under that brilliant starlit sky, and made their way down the old fisherman's pier.

When they reached the end, Lorelei looked at her brother. The last two rolls of cash held tightly in their fists.

"Ready?" she asked him.

"I'm ready," he said, smiling brighter than the moon above them.

"Me first? Or you?" he asked.

"Together," she said. "On the count of three."

She smiled, and he took a deep breath.

"One! Two! Three!" they shouted and tossed the last two rolls with all their might far into the wide, wide ocean.

"That's for you, Bentfork! No more trailer!" the young man shouted.

"Take that, Papa. And your lousy gun, too!" she yelled.

"And your nasty breath!" Beeker hollered. He held the railing tightly. "I'm worth it," he yelled.

"For Mama! Dying too young! Dying all around. I miss you so." She stood on the railing's bottom rung and screamed up to the heavens above. "And Aunt Adelaide! I'm sorry I never knew. I never knew."

"I'm here!" he shouted, bent over backward. "I! Am! Here!" He stood strong, shaking his fist to the moon.

"Come and get me world! I can take it!" she hollered to the distant waves in joyful release.

"I can take it!" he added beside her.

"You hear that, moon?" she shouted above. "We can take it!"

Shouting and laughing together in unison, breathless and energized, chests heaving and eyes wet, they released all of their anger and fear into the twilight above them and into the deep ocean below. The waves continued their rhythmic call and they began to listen.

Breathing in unison, wide-eyed in wonder, their transport had passed.

They stood silently, brother and sister, and stared at each other in breathless recognition.

She nodded her head. "We can take it," she said.

"No more handouts," he replied, and nodded in agreement. Though the silence around them was deafening, the waves reminded them both of the journey still ahead.

"You ready?" she asked.

"I am," he said.

"Let's get to work then," Lorelei said, her sincere eyes shining with new light she didn't know was possible. As she stepped down from the railing, she knew that when her feet finally touched the earth, their journey would be one of repairing what they had lost when their parents died too young. What they fought when their dreams were drowned in the muddy waters of Kentucky, and mostly, what lay ahead, in the sugar and spice jars of a small bakery on the edge of town.

Night had fallen over Cobweb Corners, and there was one more repair to make. She knew that journey would be the most difficult of all, for she knew she had hurt a man harder than a frozen sea.

And across the globe, on the other side of the world, the sun was rising. A young woman in a cafe looked over her coffee to a stranger whose smile was warm and gentle. "Welcome to Paris," he said, his accent rich and welcoming. He saw the stranger's joyful tears and felt kinder because of them. He added, "It's going to be a beautiful day, Madame."

"Yes it is," Tori replied, beaming. "Oh yes it is." She took another sip of her rich coffee. "Thank you," shad said, and soon, she got down to the business of beginning her life.

Chapter 22

Beginnings can bring the wanderer to open roads of great possibilities. The heart leaps with each new imagined road, whether it's a midnight flight across the wide ocean, or a stormy escape in a VW bug with a hound, a backpack, and a hopeful heart.

Endings, however, are always created at a choice in the forest. No matter which path is taken, it will lead the traveler though a difficult journey where the discovery can be more important than the road's end.

Rapunzel had to lie about her prince.

Even Cinderella went undercover to the ball.

And Lorelei met her wolf.

She was not surprised to see it looked a lot like herself, and that was the loneliest journey of them all.

Yet Little Red grew empowered when she strayed from the path. Right?

So! Repair! Begin!

The story can start again, but this time without armor. Guided only by the wind, the girl with flowers in her hair took a journey every day for the next week.

Each night after dinner, she would arrange the butter, flour, and brown sugar while her brother cleaned the plates. She'd write recipes for that evening's bake, and he'd review it with her approval. She'd put on her white shoes. He'd tie on his white apron.

And both went to work.

Beeker's path was one of growth and discovery, and he wasn't lonely. He was learning how to appreciate the solitude around him, guiding him to add more lemon and browned butter, or less sugar and a dash more salt to the icing. As the weeks progressed, his path grew abundantly and for the first time in his life, he found the joy in the presence of his sister's gentle hand, the stillness around him—and baking.

Lorelei's path was always the same. Guided by her sorrowful heart, she knew she had to make amends to the man she hurt—and she, too, would hurt from that journey's inevitable end.

The road was so beautiful for a time.

Aided by her white Keds, she'd walk the half mile up the beach to the lighthouse. She'd pry open the loose plywood over the rear window, remove her shoes and place them against the wall, as though the owner magically stepped through the stone, leaving two white shoes to be the only indication of her corporeal existence.

Then, barefoot, she would swing her legs over the old sill, and with a humph, drop into the cool room beneath.

She'd sit and wait in that cool chamber, frozen in time, as the sunset spread its warm October glow over town.

Each night when it got too dark to see and she knew he would not show, she'd clamber up the wall to that same upper window—helped along the way with ladder made from a rotting couch that bore little resemblance to Rapunzel's tresses. She'd sit on the dark window ledge for a moment longer.

And she'd wait.

Every night for a week, she'd wait.

When she was convinced no man would venture out into the dark, she'd put on her white shoes, size six, and begin the journey back to a bakery, a brother, and another thousand combinations for bakes given to her by the saline scented air.

Sorrowful, but determined to continue along.

Upon her return, she'd pat Bear's solid head, tie on an apron, and not say a word to Beeker. He knew her heart was hurting. So they, brother and sister, united in dough, batter, and icing, got to work preparing delights for the town.

On the eighth evening, as Lorelei approached the lighthouse she saw the door standing open.

Was it in invitation?

Or perhaps an ogre's trap? A gingerbread witch's temptation? Or an opportunity to battle? She looked up to the sky and saw a solitary man standing on the parapet's edge, looking down upon her.

So. Begin.

"Chase?" she called.

No answer.

"Chase, can I talk with you?" she called loudly, her voice carried on the wind.

"Door's open," was the simple, flat reply.

An invitation?

Or, was it a confrontation with the ugliest mirror of them all. Her own ability to injure those she loved.

Lorelei stared at that door a long while before crossing the threshold. Heart pounding, this was the journey toward a heartbreak she never wanted to know.

She walked up the circular iron stairs knowing she had to confront the pain she had caused. Betrayal was bitter and she knew the taste all too well. However, this was something more acrid and caustic. She had been the reason for the pain, and the bile she swallowed reminded her that she was the only one who could undo the hurt.

The stairs grew tighter as she reached the top, and ironically, a bit brighter too. As she rose from the dark pillar of the lighthouse body to the housing of the gargantuan safety light, she arrived at the room of windows and light.

And one single door.

He stood on the parapet with his back to her. His elbows on the railing, he looked like a man resigned to a life alone, and confident in that decision.

"Chase?" she asked.

Silence.

"Chase, can I talk to you?" She was cautious, like she was talking to a wounded pup—or an angry lion. It was hard to tell the difference.

"You didn't climb those steps just for the view. Might as

well talk," came the stoic reply.

She stepped onto the balcony and listened for the wind to guide her, but the air was still. She knew she was on her own.

"Chase, I'm sorry," she began. "I did something horrible and I hurt you."

No reply. Just the distant beating of the gentle waves and a few gulls calling to the air.

"Uh huh," he said. His back was to her, and though still, it was stronger than the bricks and mortar of the lighthouse that held them both.

"Aren't you going to talk with me?"

"Nothing to say. You deceived me, lied, then took off for a week without a word. I've got nothing."

"Can I at least explain to you? Would you listen?" she asked with the sincerity of a truly broken heart.

"Go ahead. I'm listening."

"Chase, I'm not talking to your back. I know I was awful, but you gotta look at me at least."

When he turned to face her, she knew that it was one of the hardest journeys he had to take. His face was tight with the pain he had known before. Fran was gone and the pain was receding. But Lorelei saw she reminded him that dragons can emerge from the darkness and there was no way to kill them other than face to face combat.

On a tower.

At sunset.

Poised on the edge of the world.

He spoke first. "What do you have to say?"

"I lied. I'm sorry, Chase."

"I'll say. You could have gotten me in a hell of a mess." He turned to face the ocean. "Already did I guess."

She took a few steps toward the railing a few feet from his side and spoke to him. "Chase, when I drove here my first night, I was a kid with a dog, a dying car, and a sack of money like I never knew before. I had to kill my brother, kill the trailer, kill Kentucky just to survive."

"You killed a lot more than that."

"I know. What I did was wrong in so many ways, but I had to survive. I was stupid. I had to get out." She paused a moment and looked at the solid man next to her. "I'm not asking for you to forgive me, to like me. I just want the opportunity to explain a little. Maybe you can understand. Maybe," she said. The hope was dying in her chest.

"Go on." He said, staring into the horizon.

"Chase, my life in Kentucky sucked. I mean it sucked. My papa loved his gun and booze more than his kids. He even slept with his shotgun. And my mama? She died before she could do anything about it. Beeker was scared his whole life, so no wonder he took after my daddy. Easier to escape that kind of life than to look it in the eye and fight it."

"I fight it," he said tightly. "I fight it every day."

"You're also a strong man. Beeker isn't."

"That's not what I'm talking about."

"Chase," she said softly, "I know what you're talking about. Really. Grief stays with us forever. For some reason, our lives have carved out a special place of hurt for us both. And I think I hurt you all the more because of that. I know I did."

"That's right," he said through compressed lips.

"I'm sorry, Chase. I didn't mean to do that. I didn't even mean to steal Beeker's money. It was like all of a sudden I was staring at thousands in cash that I never even knew about. I was so angry. So, I reached in and took some. Well, a lot. Figured he owed it to me." She took a breath and continued. "I didn't mean to lie about him. It started with one simple thing and just grew like an awful beanstalk, and no matter where I looked, I couldn't find a way down."

He looked squarely into her face. "Honesty could help."

"Chase! You're stronger than I am. You're tough and you have options I never had. All I had was angry parents, a drug selling brother too lazy to do anything else, and a dead trailer that leaked so bad when it rained we could drown in the puddles. Rusted so bad, you could see the muddy water flowing under it. You have a life."

"No. I had a life. *Had*." He looked away from her, lost in the distant memories he held tightly in his pocket.

Lorelei stopped. She leaned against the thick glass behind her, wishing the lighthouse would illuminate so brightly, her soul would evaporate into the air above her. Both had reached an impasse. Blocked by pain, obstructed by heartbreak, the path before them both grew dim.

"Lorelei, for the first time in a long while," he began, "I let myself fall."

She felt small in his eyes.

"I really did." He looked at her. "I fell for you. And that's what's so awful."

"Chase, please." She knew this was going to hurt.

"No, it is awful. 'Go on dates!' my buddies told me. Hell, Connor even talked me into a dating site! But it all felt so wrong. Even Sophie. I tried a date with Sophie, and man, was that a disaster." He laughed a little at the memory. "Then I met you and it was like— Well, you're like nobody I ever met before. You know that?" He looked at her for acknowledgement. "You're this small bundle of— I don't know. Something scary and wonderful and weird and exciting and no matter how I try, I can't leave it alone." He paused a moment before he confessed. "I saw you, ya know."

"What?"

"All week long, I saw you here."

"Why didn't you talk to me?"

"Couldn't." He turned away and faced the ocean. "I was too angry, too hurt. I couldn't talk. I had to let it be done. Finished."

"Chase, all you did was prolong the inevitable. The hurt just grows more that way."

"I'm real good at that," he said. "Prolonging the inevitable."

"What does that mean?"

"It means you took off—"

"Chase, from what I remember, you took off first. That night I turned to explain to you, and you were gone."

"Lorelei! I'm a cop! Out of nowhere some strange guy shows up, says he's your twin brother. You have a sack of cash in your hands that you said is drug money! Drug money! Do you even know what that means? What the hell do you think I do for a living? Rescue cats? I took off so I didn't have to hear any more incriminating evidence. Next thing I know, you go missing. Figured you drove back home."

"This is my home, Chase. I'm not going anywhere."

"Sure looked like you took off."

"I stayed with Sophie. She took me in for a while."

"I know that now, but then? Lorelei. I can't do it."

"Can't do what?"

"Abandonment."

"What? Chase, you took—"

"Lorelei! Listen to what I'm trying to say here. This is hard. I've locked myself away from people for a long time and this kind of thing is really hard for me, okay? You took off. That's what I mean. I can't do another escape act like that."

"Chase, I'm not following. We both took off."

"No. No we didn't. You left for a week without a single word. That's what I mean! I was worried sick about you. Had no idea where you were. I can't do it Lorelei, I can't."

"Can't do what?"

"Fran! Aren't you listening? That year, those last months, I'd sit in the patrol car outside the house and pray 'one more day, just one more day, please God, one more day.'"

"I'm sorry."

"So, I learned real good how to prolong the inevitable. And all along, I knew we were barreling down this road waiting for the crash. Funny thing is, Fran never looked at it that way. A crash." His voice was shaking.

Lorelei was silent. She let him empty his grief into the night air.

"She comforted me more that I comforted her. And that's what kills me. Looking back? She was the strong one."

"Chase, you're—"

"No. Don't say it. She was the strong one. Always was. So. After? I would go home, sit in the driveway and stare at that one empty light I'd leave on, too scared to go inside that empty house." He paused, trying to get the words in place. "I'd call up Connor, fake it, like everything was fine, and meet him for dinner. Over and over and over. Then, this one night," he looked directly at Lorelei, "I saw these two white sneakers stuck in a window, waving like hell in the dark. It was like a surrender flag." He smiled a bit, enjoying the image. "Never laughed so hard in my life. And at that moment, I surrendered I guess. And that's what makes it all so hard."

"What?"

"This. I can't do it Lorelei. I'm sorry."

"Bullshit."

"What?"

"That's bullshit and you know it. Toughen up! I'm sorry but that's the way it is. You hurt, I hurt, hell the whole world hurts. Look around you. But Chase, you gotta stop living in your hurt. I get it now. Fran is gone. I took off. But I'm here now and I'm sorry. I know I hurt you. I know I made you remember painful things. But Chase, for cryin' out loud, stop living for that lonely light in your living room."

"I'm not—"

"Yes, you are! Fran even told you to fall in love again. Do you know what that even means? What she said? That woman loved you so much, she knew what your love is worth."

"Stop—"

"No way. I'm fighting for my life here. Chase! She knew! She had it. She's the only one who got it right. That kind of love isn't something to mourn and lock away. It's something you should be shouting about! Go on! Tell everyone! That's what it's all about. It's what scared my daddy so much he drowned it in a bottle. It's what Beeker was so scared of he nearly followed my daddy. But as sure as my name is Lorelei Bradley, I am not giving this up without a fight. Toughen up cop-man. I love you, and I know I hurt you, and for that I am so so sorry, but Chase, you gotta open up. Even your wife told you that."

He stood in front of her, heart beating more rapidly than the waves below their feet, and Lorelei saw the fear in his face.

"Chase. Did you hear me? I love you."

"Yeah, I heard you."

"I love you," she said again simply. "Now you can either take a chance on it, or you can walk away. But you gotta choose Chase."

"But—"

"Chase! What? If you don't talk to me how can we reach anything?"

"The flowers."

"What flowers—?"

An arched eyebrow was his only reply.

"Oh. The flowers," she said simply. She took a deep breath and told him. "Chase. I don't know what to say. It happens." And she shrugged.

She shrugged!

"But Lorelei, I saw you get lost in a blizzard of flowers! From nowhere ... That seemed to come from—"

"My hair?" She smiled broadly.

"Your hair." He was suddenly quiet.

"Yep. That's about right I guess."

"What? That's it? That's the best reason you have? 'Oh sometimes a thousand flowers just grow from my hair. Want a cupcake?' That's it."

Lorelei laughed. "Chase," she said. "Yeah. That's it. I told you I get my recipes from the wind. Did you think I was making that up?"

"I thought it was a metaphor," he said dryly.

She laughed, hard. "No. No, that's where I really get the ideas. The wind. Always been like that too. My aunt knew. You've seen the bakery. Ever wonder why there aren't any cookbooks?"

"Aunt Adelaide knew and I think she was trying to teach me about all of it. She came down when my mama was dying and looking back, she knew. She must have had it too. She'd look at me so deeply, with such love it was scary. I never saw love like that before. Ever. But she had it, and I guess she saw I did too. She gave me more than I could ever repay."

"And?" He was tentative.

"And what?"

"Lorelei! The flowers. What was that?"

"That, my friend, is part of the package."

He looked dubious. "Part of the package—"

She turned to him. "Chase. Aren't you listening to me? What I'm offering you. I fell in love with you. I am in love with you! And yes, part of the package is that I listen to the wind and from time to time, things occur that I choose not to explain to myself or to anyone. It's much easier to accept it and let it happen."

She suddenly became all mock-scientific, bunching her

shoulders up like a lab assistant, "Rather than to dive in and get it all diagnosed and figured and explained. What good would that do? What purpose does logic serve anyway, other than to dim what little magic we have left in this world. So. Do you accept?"

"Accept?"

She let out a playful exasperated scream. "Your one word answers are going to drive me insane! Listen to me. I want to be in love with you. I want to be with you! And yes, from time to time, you need to accept some magic too. 'Bout time if you asked me."

He stared at her, wonder in his eyes, heart full of the impish woman in front of him, and said simply, "I guess so. Yes. I'm in Lala. I'm in."

Without a second thought, Lorelei threw herself at him and tossed her arms around his massive chest. She covered his face and neck with the warmest kisses he had ever felt. "Oh Chase, my Chase," she said, lost between catching her breath, and the abundant kisses she gave him. He, too, melted into this most fantastic of all embraces. The joining of lost lovers, the reunion of potential and future combined, and heartbeats in perfect sync and rhythm.

The kisses they shared one hundred fifty-six feet in the air, two hundred and fourteen steps above the beach, reminded them of what they nearly lost and what they had found. Each breath, each soft brush of their lips made up for lost time—a week, a year, a lifetime—and they began to rewrite the book that told them that existence was a lonely thing.

In its place, where they thought their roads would end, they found only love and as the pages opened up before them, they began to write their own beautiful endings, in icing and ink.

Part 4: Late Fall

Decorate with Sugar Roses

Chapter 23

Residents in town can tell the changing of the seasons by the glorious foliage display as much as by the handful of tourists who linger a week or two beyond the golden glow of the oak and fire red shades of the ample maple trees.

Two Falls flourished and passed through Cobweb Corners since that kiss above the ocean, and like a sweet ballet, left romantic dreams lingering in the air to carry the viewers through another cold New England winter.

When Adelaide turned one, Lorelei and Chase threw a small birthday party for their daughter on the beach, just below his grandfather's silent lighthouse. It had grown a bit grayer, a bit dustier, but it was still filled with the promise of its solid brick holding fast to the earth's core below, and the potential of discovery reaching into the consistent blue skies above.

Chase held the baby in his arms and surveyed all that surrounded him. Grateful for his good fortune, he watched as Connor loaded plates with steamers and crabs. Connor was a lucky man. Chase enjoyed watching his friend command the fire pit—total guy territory, and he loved it. His wife, Keighley, handed out napkins and small cups loaded with melted butter and garlic, and every now and then, she'd lay a soft hand upon her stomach, caressing the new soul unfurling within.

A loud laugh shook his attention to another corner of the party. Sophie was bent over double, howling as her husband, Tucker, shook a feisty crab from his finger into the pot, laughing in mock pain. An unlikely couple, but Chase also knew love when he saw it, and Sophie's eyes illuminated it abundantly. Tucker froze for a moment when he saw his wife's eyes. He mumbled a few words to her, smiling wider than the sea itself, and Chase saw Sophie's posture melt a bit, her eyes shining brilliantly in the firelight. Then, something remarkable happened. Sophie walked gently toward this man she fell in love with. She wrapped her arms around Tucker, whispered something in his ear, and then, they began a slow dance to the tune of the waves around them, and the joyful meter of company celebrating his daughter's birth.

A pair of eyes caught his attention.

Lorelei.

His breath caught in his throat. She was so beautiful, this magical woman with flowers in her hair. He realized that abundance was everywhere. That sorrows were just stones we were taught to keep in our pockets by angry, frightened men.

He smiled broadly that night. Looking at his wife, holding his daughter in his strong capable arms, he became thankful for the journey that led him to this, the most remarkable of all journeys. A love, a life, and a daughter.

Adelaide struggled a bit in his arms. "Hey baby girl," he cooed. "How's my birthday girl?" His voice was warm and comforting as he lifted her against his chest and rested her head on his shoulder. He smiled when he caught Lorelei watching him in this incredible role. A dad.

He winked at her and buried his face into his daughter's soft check and nibbled a bit. Adelaide giggled and squirmed and soon, against her father's peppery warm chest, she fell asleep.

He loved the smell of her. Why had no one ever told him how babies smell so sweet? Like warm milk and powder and tangy soft? He nuzzled her again and felt something small and soft stick to his lip. He brushed it away with his hand, and there, held between his thick finger and thumb, was a tiny, delicate flower.

He looked at Lorelei, who saw, too. She waited to see what he would do.

He looked at Beeker, sitting contented in the sand, a sleeping hound in his lap.

He looked at his friends illuminated by the warm fire he built with his own hands.

And then he looked at his daughter and the tiny flower on his thumb.

Though his life took paths that led him to painful places, he discovered an abundance of love surrounding him.

When he looked up at Lorelei, he felt whole and complete in her gaze and knew their journey together was just beginning. So, this is love.

"Hi," he said simply.

"Hey," she returned, softer than poetry.

Frances DeleCourt Winters

Frances DeleCourt Winters teaches Victorian literature at a small university in Pennsylvania, and spends the summers in a mountain community in rural northern New Jersey. When not reading the most recent romance novel or writing creative fiction, Frances works on restoring a Victorian farmhouse from its skeletal stone foundation to its original gilded gingerbread trim.

You might also enjoy . . .

Frances DeleCourt Winters

A novel full of life, love—and just a hint of magic!

The Fortune Teller's Garden

www.ingramcontent.com/pod-product-compliance
Lightning Source LLC
Chambersburg PA
CBHW070750180626
46818CB00007B/3057